The Alphabet Garden

The Alphabet Garden

EUROPEAN SHORT STORIES

Edited by Pete Ayrton

SERPENT'S TAIL

These translations received financial support from the Commission of the European Communities, Brussels

Library of Congress Catalog Card Number: 94-67027

A catalogue record for this book is available from the British Library on request

These stories are works of fiction. Any resemblance to persons living or dead is purely coincidental

The quotation on page 153 from *Griechenland*, by Friedrich Hölderlin, translated by Michael Hamburger, is used by kind permission of Anvil Press

First published 1994 by
Serpent's Tail, 4 Blackstock Mews, London N4 and
401 West Broadway #1, New York, NY 10012

Typeset in 11pt Bembo by Servis Filmsetting Ltd, Manchester
Printed in Finland by Werner Söderström Oy

Contents

This book is dedicated to
Rob van Gennep (1937–1994)
– European publisher and inspiration.

Introduction

At a time when there is a tendency to assume that the dominant corporations in film, video and books are encouraging writers to produce to a bland, homogeneous Euro-standard, it is vital to show that, on the contrary, writers are creating in their different styles and languages works with a very distinct sense of time and place. In order to be universal, good writing must be local: that is, deeply rooted in a specific culture.

The impetus for this short story collection was the Frankfurt Bookfair. We know only too well (every year articles in the press say so) that the Bookfair is where absurd amounts of champagne are drunk and thousands paid for books. However, the Bookfair is also a unique opportunity for publishers and editors from all over the world to meet and share insights on the state of contemporary fiction, tips on this year's 'hot' list and complain about the nefarious effect of literary prizes. Over the years, it has become clear to me that what you get out of the Bookfair depends on what you put into it and that existing networks of contacts and friends can be put to good use.

At the 1992 Bookfair, a group of publishers from twelve different European countries met and decided that:

– each of them would commission a writer from their country to write a short story.

– the stories would be translated by all the other publishers and the resulting book would be published simultaneously in the twelve countries during the 1994 Frankfurt Bookfair. The result is *The Alphabet Garden.*

Working together on the book has been an instructive and rewarding experience. If the book goes some way to show the richness and variety of European cultures, it will have achieved its aim – by no means a modest one.

Pete Ayrton

UNITED KINGDOM

A Bit of a Tease

MICHÈLE ROBERTS

My name? That depends on where I'm working. I'm Annunciata in Italy, Joan in England, Danielle in France, Dolores in Spain, Hildegarde in Germany, and so on. These international hotels are so alike, I forget where I am sometimes! Here, in this country, my name is–

Oh, sorry.

I'm talking too fast? You don't understand. Silly me. What's that?

You want to call me Patricia. I remind you of your mother? Oh really. That's fine by me. Pleased to meet you I'm sure.

Yes I'd love to join you in a drink. What have you got in there? Whisky. That'll do me fine.

(He used to call me his little bear. That was his pet name for me. That and Elfin Ears. He used to hold me by the tops of my ears and pull them upwards, to make the tips even more pointed. I didn't mind him teasing me. I adored him, didn't I. I sat on his knee and pretended to be his teddy-bear.)

It's a funny job this one. You meet all sorts. Take yourself. Meaning no offence of course. All kinds. University professors, taxi drivers, shop assistants, they all come to me. Or I go to them. It depends. Riff-raff too, always supposing they've got the money. I prefer cash, did I tell you that, and I do like people to be clean, no smelly crotches or stained trousers, please. Apart from that I don't care. I'm not a snob. I'll look after a bishop or a Member of Parliament or a bank clerk, I'm not fussy. Word gets around if you're good at the job, if you know how to treat people well. That's what counts. People recommend me to their friends. Or I'm hired by the organization, like today.

Dear me, listen to me rabbiting on. You're much too polite to say so, but I can tell from your face you've only understood one word in three of what I'm saying.

Sorry. I will talk more slowly. You are a foreigner. I should not expect you to understand my language. In your country I would not be able to speak yours.

(He and I didn't use words much. We didn't need to. One glance at his face when he came in and I knew straight away what he was feeling. I concentrated on him. I learned him. By heart and in silence. It was our secret. He called it that. Our secret, Elfin Ears. So that *she* wouldn't guess, couldn't find out.)

Where was I. Oh yes. This job's not quite what I was brought up to, I can tell you. But I relish it, the oddness of it, in relation to what I could have been, oh I don't know, a chiropodist or a dental nurse or a hospital receptionist. The kind of thing I was expected to be. Daddy working in a hospital all his life, naturally he wanted his only child to follow in his footsteps. Well, I've stayed in what they call the caring professions haven't I. You can't get much more caring than this! You probably didn't expect to find someone like me doing this, did you. Well now, I'll tell you something that will really surprise you. Neither did I!

Finished your whisky have you? Oh right. Right then. Let's get down to business shall we. That's what we're both here for after all. Let's get this show on the road.

Don't ask me to translate that! I haven't a clue!

Listen, lovey, I'm not here to chat. Well, not *only* to chat.

That's right. Just slip them off. I'll put them here for you, over the back of this chair. No rush. Take your time.

(He was a big man. The sort I've preferred ever since, that you can get your arms comfortably around, sink into and on to. I can't stand skinny men. For a start it's not in the least bit sensual, all those bony bits sticking out, and secondly thin men always make me feel inadequate somehow, because I'm so much plumper than they are. They look at me disapprovingly, and I know they're thinking I'm too fat. I like a man with some flesh on him, something to knead and nuzzle and sniff. He was big, and tall with it. Seeing him without his clothes on always made me smile with delight. There was so much of him to enjoy. Bedtime now, I'd whisper. Daddy put your little girl to bed.)

When I began this work, you know, when I discovered I had a real calling for it, I could only think how shocked my family would be if they found out. But that's all past now. I don't need anyone's approval of what I do and I don't ask for it. I make a good living and I'm content. Everyone lives by their purse, their wallet, don't they. That's what you have to think of. The only thing that matters really.

It's not like that for you? No? Perhaps because you've got enough. You must be one of the lucky ones. I should have guessed, shouldn't I, seeing as you're staying in this deluxe four-star hotel! Now let me see. Let me see if I can guess. A stockbroker perhaps? A sales director? A lawyer?

You make books. Oh I see, you're a publisher.

Sorry but I don't get it.

Oh, a writer. An *author*.

You're attending the international publishing conference in this hotel? Oh I see. That must be nice. So what kind of books do you write? Novels. Right. What are they about, your novels? Autobiographical, are they? I've often thought I should like to write a novel, if only I had the time.

(Our best time together was in the bed he shared with her, one afternoon while she was out. That made it more exciting, the risk we were taking, the danger we'd be found out if she came home early. Possibly I wanted to be caught doing it. With him. Yes, that's probably true. The other exciting thing was the smell of the sheets. He didn't bother changing them first, we were in too much of a hurry. They were rumpled and warm, and they smelled of him, his night warmth, his sweat. They smelled of her too, oh yes, and afterwards there was a new smell added. Mine. Ever since that day I've loved sex in the afternoons, the sunlight glowing through the drawn blinds, being able to see him so easily, not feeling sleepy, drunk on touching not on wine.)

So. Why don't you come and lie down. That's it. Make yourself comfortable. On your back to start with I think. On the couch, as one of my recent clients put it. That was when I was working for this international congress of psychoanalysts recently. This guy, American I admit but still, he charged people $200 a session just to tell him their problems. Can you believe that! What I'm doing, I told him, is more effective, quicker, and costs far less. Because I don't charge a lot, when I'm working back at home, seeing individual clients, if people can't pay. It's a sort of vocation, doing this. I've discovered I've got a gift, so I don't believe in exploiting the people who come to me in need. That psychoanalyst, I had him sorted out in no time.

That's it. Lie back.

You're following me? I'm sorry I keep forgetting to speak slowly. I get carried away! So will you quite soon I hope.

Now just relax.

(Right from the start I was a complete sucker for married men. The taboo thing, I suppose. That, and then the fact that the ending was built in. I discovered when I was quite young that I didn't want to be tied down. I liked having affairs. I liked moving on. Recreational sex they call it now. I called it having a strong sex drive. Comes to the same thing. It means not pretending every time that you've fallen in love. It's about honesty. Non-monogamy they called it in the seventies. It's not only men who like it. Plenty of women do too only they mostly won't admit it. My mother called it being a bit of a slut. And *she*, when she found out, as of course she was bound to do, because I made sure she would sooner or later, she had no words for it at all.

He was the best I've had. And yes, he was the first. He was the family doctor. It was so easy just to turn up, late afternoons, in his surgery. For a long time no one suspected a thing. *She* did, after all she worked as his receptionist, but she couldn't bear to face what she was thinking.

I was thirteen, and he was fifty. That day, I saw he couldn't believe his luck. I was very pretty, so young, with a flawless body. I threw myself at him. Let's say I made myself available. He did his best to please me to the utmost. Oh, the bliss he gave me. Over and over again.

I remember how gently his fingers slid in. With his voice he pretended that this was just a routine, let's have a look at you then he said, but his fingers couldn't lie. They trembled as they touched my skin, then ever so gently he parted my lips and slid his fingers in. I was so wet, his fingers swam in me. Neither of us said a word. On his face was terror, the beginning of delight, lust, tenderness. I'd made him feel all those things. I was slippery with it, my power over him, warm and swollen and slippery. I could smell my sex, and I could smell his. I stared at him. Silently I dared him to move his hand. He began to stroke me then, very carefully, as though I were precious to him. And at the same time he gabbled out a lot of medical nonsense for the benefit of anyone who might be trying to listen through the door.)

That psychoanalyst had the cheek to say *he'd* like to help *me*. He said we'd have to swap places and I'd have to talk. He said he helped people cope with their problems by getting them to talk about their sexual fantasies from their traumatic childhoods. Mine was very happy, thank you, and as you can see I'm fine at talking, I have no problems with that. Keeping up a gentle flow of chat can be useful in this job, with the shy clients. Mmmm? As is being on the tall side. That's very useful, with all the lifting and turning and so on. Especially with the *and so on*! And a couple of times I've had to restrain a client when he got over-excited. It helps having some muscles, a bit of height.

But you're not going to want me to get rough with you are you. You're the gentle sort. One of the shy ones aren't you. It's the way you jumped a second ago when I turned down the lights. Don't worry. I'm used to you shy ones. You're a challenge, someone like you.

Do you understand what I'm saying? I'm telling you not to worry. I respect how you feel. You're nervous aren't you.

It's your first time isn't it.

Your first time.

That's deeply exciting for me too.

I wouldn't dream of laughing at you. I'm here to help. Easy does it. That's my philosophy. One step at a time.

(The way I began it was like this. Well, he began it too. I went to see him first of all with a bit of a cough. He was new then in the district, the old GP had just retired, and I never went to the doctor normally, I was a very healthy child. I saw him driving past our house one day, oh there's the new doctor my mother exclaimed, he's so handsome isn't he, and *so* kind. She'd already had an appointment of course, you could trust her not to be slow off the mark.

I sat on the couch, turned away from him. He pulled up my shirt to stethoscope my back. His fingers brushed over my bra strap, and he grunted. Without saying a word he undid the hook and eye fastening, then he went on putting the cold metal end of his instrument here and there all over my back. Then he turned me round to face him. His white coat was close to my face. It was glossy with starch and ironing, stiff as white card. He smelled of soap, and some sharp lemony aftershave, and another smell, deeper than these, which was just him. His fingernails were clipped short, and were very clean. That was what I liked, how clean he was, and yet how he smelled of warm animal, just faintly sweaty, as though he'd been running. He unbuttoned the front of my shirt, pulled my bra up, above my breasts, and stethoscoped me some more. Then he showed me how to examine my breasts. His hands on me were so light and cool, I thought I'd faint with pleasure. I could see my nipples poking forwards like raspberries. Wetness gushed between my legs. I knew he could smell it. He smiled at me and asked me how long since my periods began and whether they caused me any trouble. Might as well give you a proper check-up while you're here, he remarked. He told me to lie down.

He didn't undress me completely or tell me to undress myself. I suppose in case anyone came in. He slid his hands up under my skirt, into the top of my knickers, out again. As though he were absent-minded, as though he weren't really doing it at all, he caressed me through the thin cotton, all the while talking about I don't know what, a healthy diet I think it was, until I was really wet. I felt so swollen up down there, like a balloon ready to explode. And then he pulled my knickers down to my knees, and then down to my ankles, keeping them there so that my feet were twined together, but my knees were wide apart, he pushed them open and told me to keep them that way. Be a good girl, he whispered. Let me help you. Just trust me.)

When you're ready. First of all you've got to trust me and

that takes time. That's what you're paying for after all. Someone you can trust. I'm very patient you know. I don't expect results in five minutes and nor should you. On the other hand fifty minutes is fifty minutes and I don't want to waste any of this precious time!

No, I can't translate all that. I can hardly speak a word of your language, you must have realized that by now.

Look, listen to what my hands are telling you. I'm talking to you through my fingertips. Surely you can understand *that*.

Let me just adjust that towel a second. I don't want you catching cold and going all gooseflesh. It seems very warm in here to me, lovely efficient central heating they have in this country don't they, but you still look as though you're shivering. There now. Nice and comfy are we? All wrapped up in super thick soft towels. There. Now you're all tucked in. Mummy's baby. Mummy's best boy.

In a minute I'll put a tape on. You can choose which one. Just a sec while I open this.

I'm warming a few drops of this oil in the palms of my hands so it will feel nice and warm on your skin. Can you smell it? Citrus and juniper I've picked out for you, with just a hint of carnation and a smidgeon of sandalwood. A combination of energizing and relaxing. Lovely fragrance isn't it? It'll make you feel less tense. Just you wait and see.

(At first I was a little tense. I couldn't believe what was happening. Come upstairs, he whispered. She's out all afternoon playing bridge. In the bedroom he took me in his arms, kissing me deeply, jamming me against his crotch. I felt his hardness through the cloth of his trousers. He unzipped himself so that I could touch him. He was so warm. So alive. He pushed me on to the bed. We lay head to tail and licked each other, I nibbled and sucked on him as though I were starving, and he stopped exploring me with his tongue and groaned aloud. Then his head came up and his hands and he spun me round to face him again and drove his fingers inside me, caressing and rubbing until I was whimpering. Fuck me, I whispered. Fuck me fuck me fuck me. At the same time I was listening for her step on the stairs. It drove me wild, the idea that she might come in and find us there.)

I'll start with your feet and work upwards from there, all right? I'll uncover just one little bit of you at a time, to spare your blushes!

You'd think I'd get bored, wouldn't you, performing the same gestures over and over again every day. But with every client it's as though it's the first time all over again. The thing is, you have to get to know the client a little bit first, to work out what he'll like, or she of course. What will suit.

Which reminds me. A tape! Here they are. Now which one would you like to hear? I've got versions in all the major European languages. Including yours of course. Confessions of a Vicarage Maiden, Lesbian Teenage Love Romp, Lolita and the GP, Kinky Housewife Sluts, er, let's see.

You'd like Lolita and the GP? Fine. Here we go then. Now, back to your feet. Your lovely long toes. My goodness they do like being attended to, don't they. Positively thrusting themselves into my hands.

Sssh now. Lie back and listen while I get on with my job.

He used to call me his little bear. That was his pet name for me. That and Elfin Ears. He used to hold me by the tops of my ears and pull them upwards, to make the tips even more pointed. I didn't mind him teasing me. I adored him, didn't I. I sat on his knee and pretended to be his teddy-bear.

DENMARK

The Alphabet Garden

IB MICHAEL

translated by Joan Tate

1

I have visited a house called oblivion.

It is in the garden just opposite, and from my roof terrace I can see the shadows of the treetops playing over the paths. This garden was created by Maximilian, the unhappy Archduke from Austria and his wife Carlotta. He inherited an empire in Mexico and found himself on a cactus throne. The garden is surrounded by a man-high wall over which bougainvillea flow like breakers in a dream-coloured sea.

Single cypresses wave their brushes beneath the sky and orchids glow in the foliage.

Maximilian originally took over a country house as a sanctuary he made for himself and his Belgian princess. Opposite is a country church, and to the left a store full of dusty merchandise.

The entrance to the botanical gardens is through the gateway of the hacienda. The old buildings are being restored. One of the wings had served as a stable for Maximilian's imported horses, Arab thoroughbreds, befitting a man from one of the most ancient royal houses of Europe.

The souvenir stall inside sells a photograph of his black carriage outside the entrance, the ears of the mules laid back. On this yellowing photograph, the walls have taken on the colour they have in reality. You can see that the entrance is the same – with its lattice gate and slanting tiled roof shading the iron door.

At first you come to a wishing well in which the coins glint with all their confidence in the water. Further on down the path, you come to a clump of copal trees and if you poke at the bark a little it smells like a church. That is the white resin that has been sweated out by the sun, the resin burnt on the altars of pyramid temples, and then in Spanish churches. Humming-birds fly between the leaves, the hum of their wings coming from their invisible suspension between heaven and earth.

Then the garden begins to divide into paths and you are taken from beds of lemon grass and aloes to a meticulously laid-out desert where all kinds of cacti have dried the air between them, so nothing but sunlight quivers in their needle-sharp thorns.

Here, over the centuries, loving couples have carved their names on the leaves, and the oldest ones have become crusted, forming scar tissue in the middle of the green. Drawn hearts, fresh or withered, pierced by arrows, they are symbols recognized everywhere.

One name seems familiar to me, but at first I pay little attention to it. Mexican names are very alike.

From this small cactus desert, through a grove of oleander trees, the path runs behind to the house Maximilian had built in the centre of his botanical garden. He called the house 'El Olvido', oblivion, but later it came to be known colloquially as 'The House of the Pretty Girl' after his lover.

Her name was Conchita. She was the daughter of the gardener and not yet eighteen when Maximilian started courting her. He was lonely. Carlotta was away. The French Emperor had betrayed him and his auxiliary troops were in retreat. The emperor of dreams was fighting for a realm that no longer existed.

In a last attempt to save the remains of an empire fading like dreams in the light of morning, the Empress had returned to Europe to seek an audience with Napoleon III of France, whose strategic abilities could easily be contained on a silk handkerchief. On the whole, he had plainly not inherited the warrior heart of his uncle, the little Corsican, and pretended illness when the Mexican adventure suddenly appeared in his apartments in the form of this determined figure of a woman. It did not suit him that the marionettes had taken on a life of their own and no longer obeyed the pull of the strings.

When Carlotta realized the adventure was over and Maximilian had been left in the lurch, she was seized with despair, which turned into a quite understandable persecution mania. From then on she thought Napoleon's agents were everywhere, trying to poison her. She travelled on to Rome, where she sought an audience with the Pope. Forgiveness was not in the minds of the men of the church and Maximilian's policies in Mexico had not lived up to expectations. Carlotta noticed that. They could expect no help from that quarter.

She refused to leave the Vatican, settled down in the Pope's highly personal apartments and thus, at least officially, became the first woman to have spent a night under the same roof as the prince of the church. A few days later, on the pretext of a drive, they lured her out and had her committed to a mental hospital. After that she was incarcerated in Château Bouchout in Belgium.

That was her final journey and she never again returned to reality. She had her moments of clarity during which she wrote letters and spoke of Napoleon as the Prince of Darkness, while she referred to her beloved Maximilian as the Lord of the Universe.

When Maximilian was informed of her destiny, they at first tried to spare him, saying her nerves were troubling her and she was receiving treatment. But he recognized the doctor's name, one of the most famous doctors of mental disorders in Europe. Once he knew the truth of the situation, he probably had some need for oblivion. He sought it in his beautiful garden, in the house where they had spent some of their happiest moments.

It is a fairly modest house and on the day I chose to visit it, the walls had just been freshened up with bright red paint. The rear, to which my steps carried me, faces on to a lawn. From a terrace where red hawthorn alternates with what we at home call Star of Bethlehem, steps go down to a pool of goldfish gliding like thoughts below the surface of the water. On both sides of the terrace, French windows lead into rooms which lie in darkness behind the panes.

I sit down in a ray of sunlight on the terrace and let my gaze roam along the paths that have brought me there. I close my eyes and imagine a time just round the corner and singing through the mirage of the siesta.

A rustle behind me, a sense of wind through leaves. I hear a voice and turn my head. Maximilian's tall figure would not have surprised me, nor would La Conchita's rustling skirts. But the voice does. For it belongs to a woman, an elderly woman with streaks in her hair, and her voice is as harsh as sandpaper.

She clears her throat.

What am I doing here, she asks me, and why haven't I come in through the front door on the other side of the house where the souvenir stall is?

I explain myself. My excitement in the presence of history in the endless rooms alongside these. I nod over towards the French windows. She looks closely at me for a moment or two before inviting me inside. There is a glass-green reflection in her eyes as she opens the doors and the smell of stone and earth pours out from the interior of the house.

Inside, everything is in semi-darkness. There are two desks and two tubular steel chairs, neither papers nor the usual spring binder on the desks, but bundles of plants, their aroma filling the room.

Herbariums and books lie on shelves round the room, tongues of paper and dried flowers protruding from them. I think that if you opened those binders and started turning the pages, they would display everything again, silent and radiant – as in a glass of water in which a Japanese paper flower is about to unfold.

After looking round the premises, I exclaim aloud. For there is not the slightest sign here of Maximilian's day. Not a piece of furniture, nor a single historical painting. No faded curtains or showcases containing pistols and swords. Not a single dusty grey example of his many Mexican hats, or his trousers with silver down the seams, his spurs, his snuff boxes and smelling salts, inkwell, his ivory paperknife, bookends, bootjacks. . .

She replies soberly. They had had no desire for a museum dedicated to a period of time that had had such an evil outcome and could still cause shudders in descendants. Not for nothing was the house to be called oblivion. So they have made it into a museum for the breeding of medicinal plants, and she is a *doctora* and a herbalist.

A subdued tone has come into her voice. She is probably imagining she is standing over a head seething with visions and sounds into which she refuses to be drawn. But if I really want to – and here she pulls out a desk drawer – then I can take a look at this photograph of Maximilian facing the firing squad.

I gape in silence at the photograph, my blood racing. For there he is, up against the wall. Crudely taken on the silver-oxydized glass plate of the day, through a lens in a brass tube. The atmosphere still there, surprisingly real – everything that happens minutes before his death, and that moment seems to come whirling out of time.

On the extreme left, half out of the frame of the photograph, is a Mexican soldier from the squad, standing to attention and so small, the bayonet on his rifle reaches a good way above his tall cap. He looks like a cowed labourer. Then come Maximilian's loyal generals, the Indian Mejia with arms folded and gaze directed defiantly at the lens of the camera, in the centre the conservative Miramon, high forehead and pointed beard, arms hanging loosely down in front of his uniform coat, one hand over the other. He is also staring straight out of the photograph.

It could have been a moment ago that Maximilian had changed places with him after pronouncing the words that were to reverberate for ever in time: 'General, a brave man should always be honoured by his emperor and in the hour of death. Allow me to take your place!', thus breaking with military order and the ranking hierarchy.

What is interesting is that of the paintings that portray the scene as the squad fires, nearly all have preserved the original grouping with the Emperor in the centre.

Because of the crude quality of the photograph, the boundary between the ground they are standing on and the wall rising behind them is invisible. They look as if they are already up in the heavens.

Maximilian is on the extreme right, in the foreground of the photo, towering in relation to the others. His coat looks dusty, but that could be the light.

He is the only one in profile. He has a crucifix raised in one hand and you can actually see that he is speaking – although his mouth is hidden by his soft beard. His childish forehead is glowing.

He is thirty-five. We know from sources what he is saying. It has been carefully prepared in Spanish, the pronunciation of which he still doesn't quite master: 'I forgive everyone and also pray that they will forgive me. May my blood be the last to flow in this country. *Que viva Mexico!*'

Words that were to be his last, but did not become so. This is what occurred:

He parted his beard and exposed his shirt front in one and

the same movement. When the salvo of shots crashed out at the sound of his 'Viva Mexico!', Maximilian fell forward, face first, buried his hands in his chest and groaned out one single word:

'*Hombres...*'

We will never know whether he meant 'men' or 'human beings', whether it was the beginning of a new sentence, an exclamation of pain, or an echo of what he had already said to the men as he had handed them gold coins. He had asked them to aim properly and not fire at his face. Struck in one eye, he groaned out that last exclamation.

The officer hurried up and turned him over, then pointed the tip of his sword at his heart and ordered one of the soldiers – I imagine the little soldier on the photograph – to fire at close range, so the coat caught fire and flames licked at the Emperor's beard.

He was lying quite still now... after the twitch of the shot to the heart, his mouth gaping vacantly while the cacophony all round him ceased.

'Human beings!' A resignation, perhaps, at the immutability of roles and the imitative force of the photograph? An appeal from the neighbouring country to those of us still alive? A last astonishing insight, words that could have changed everything? Or 'men', nothing else, like the recurring brutes of history?

I think it over as once again I live through his death and clasp my temples, a persistent pain making its way out. The photograph has turned into a negative and has fallen away from me. So they fired at his face all the same, it rumbles through me at the pace of my blood. The terrazzo floor comes rushing up, a white wall, a dazzling slash at the brain –

When I come to again, I am lying on a wooden bench with a leather cover, surrounded by an appalling smell of hide. I have a cloth across my forehead, just growing cold again. A camomile-like fluid is trickling round my nostrils: I rub at it and try to get up, like someone suddenly woken from his own embalming. A sun-wrinkled arm pushes me gently back on to the pillow she has placed on the arm of the bench.

'You see...' she mumbles, making consoling noises with her tongue. 'You see.'

Nothing else. My limbs calm down under her strangely clear gaze.

'It's the heat,' I say. 'I must have been indisposed.'

But she shakes her head and the grey streaks in her hair draw a cobweb in the chilly semi-darkness. The cold in my body makes my words echo in my ears, and I turn to the wall. A little later, I notice her hand on my shoulder with a pressure that brings back where I am into place. Then I turn my head and meet her smile with gratitude. Outside, the bells in the open tower of San Miguel church begin to ring.

2

'I'll tell you a story,' she says when the church bells have stopped ringing and the stillness has once again returned.

'A few years ago a man came to this place, a man like you with blue eyes and his head full of spontaneous dreams. But he was a Mexican, dark-skinned and with hair as black as mine was when I was young. He called himself Santos Linares, but I don't think that was his real name. I didn't ask...'

The sound of the name made one of my eyelids quiver. It was the name I had seen carved on a cactus when I had come into the garden. Together with a date I had not taken in.

She pinches my arm with sudden sharpness and I listen again:

'At first he walked round the garden for a long time, reading all the labels with the botanical names, one by one, as if they contained a personal message, or that it was important for him to learn the universal names yet again. Not until he had taken in the name did his face brighten in recognition, and he crushed the lemon-grass leaves between his fingers and sniffed at its scent. Or he peeled the skin off a fallen mango with an expression as if he were the very first person in the garden.

'Half hidden behind my window, I couldn't help being amused by him. At the same time, he touched something in me, and I dropped the curtain and, slightly ashamed, I went on with my work of classifying medicinal plants Maximilian had had planted in his day. The names were to be updated, mistakes rectified, labels rewritten, but generally speaking what he had sent for – not just from Mexico, but from all over the world – was impressive. What detailed knowledge, what a wealth of shades in his knowledge! You sensed that behind the creation of the garden was a great hovering mind. Like reading a book he had written down in codes of living plants.

'Suddenly I heard steps on the terrace. He must have come the same way as you did, Señor. As before, I got up and went out. And as before I was standing over a man who had to be woken, because he had fallen under a spell of the goldfish in a pool just like all the others. He asked for Maximilian in exactly the same way, as if he had something to contribute to history itself.

'I didn't show him the photograph. I showed him *un Milagro*. That means a Miracle, but it isn't what you think. It's a votive painting, a portrait – a miniature – of La Conchita in the bloom of her youth. Her hair is dressed with flowers. For once she is not wearing a ball dress with balloon skirts and stays, to live up to her European sisters, but is in a *Huipil* from Tehuantepec, with a coloured border. One hand is resting on a box. Her face is glowing, and the Aztec lips are curved into a secretive smile. She is with child. And like all portraits of pregnant women, there is something Mona Lisa-like about her. Unfortunately, I cannot show you it.

'These *milagros* are produced here in Mexico on the occasions of major and minor miracles. It is said that Maximilian himself painted the picture and had it put up in the church over there. In order thus to keep his hand over a pregnancy he was never to see fulfilled.

'The man who called himself Santos Linares drew it in with flaring nostrils – a faint scent of incense still hung round the miracle. He worshipped it, his lips miming a prayer. Then he turned it over and stared for a long time – as if searching for an opening on the other side through which he could penetrate more deeply into the picture.

'Suddenly he began to shake all over. He fell, his body arching up into a bow from neck to heel as he ground his teeth and jerked out sounds he could no longer control. I had a man with falling sickness on my hands...'

At those old-fashioned words, a veil had clearly crossed my face, for she hurried to explain: 'An epileptic.' And then she went on – with a no less enigmatic smile:

'I hunted like mad for the famous stick to put between his teeth, and it became a liquorice root from the garden, so effervescent it bubbled from his mouth, smelling like a children's birthday and coming out in colours! I know perfectly well that's no laughing matter, but to be honest, it was a relief. Because do you know what – The Bald One won't appear with such things when the time is in, I know that!

'And so it was. Shortly afterwards his limbs calmed down again, the cramp gave way and I managed to get him up on to the bench, where he lay sucking at it with a smile behind his closed eyes. When he came to, he was like a lost child and couldn't remember what had happened. He asked so insistently whether he might stay overnight in the house that I let him do so, good heavens, although it was with fearful forebodings I closed the garden and went back home. He wanted nothing to eat, but simply to rest after his attack.

'Early the next morning when I went back again, he had gone. The painting of La Conchita was missing, and has never been seen since. Some time afterwards I discovered that the bed planted with what the Aztecs called *Toloatzin* had been cleared. We call it *Datura stramonium* or Thorn Apple. The plant is poisonous and produces powerful visions and eventually insanity. In smaller doses, it works as a muscle relaxer.

'I was angry – he had abused my trust – and I was seized with an inner unease. I don't know how I can explain it, but I felt the alphabet had lost a letter. The very one which provided all the others with meaning. The order of the garden had been disturbed.

'I had the bed replanted, but it was never the same again. Something irreparable had happened. I went through the garden from A to Z, and there was apparently no other damage. Yes, on the label in the bed of everlasting flowers, the **a** had been altered and an **s** added so that it said Siemper viv**es**, you live for ever! It struck me as an ill-omened whisper from the other side. Then I thought about it day and night and cursed – from the depths of my insomnia – the disturber of my peace...'

She stopped abruptly.

'Go now. And do me a favour – forget what I've told you.'

Slightly perplexed, I get up off the bench. For a few confused moments the cloth with the camomile falls from my forehead down over my eyes, turning the semi-darkness green. After I have taken it off and put it down, I find I am alone. I haven't heard her going, and find my own way out.

Outside, dusk has fallen. The red and purple bougainvillea has merged into the falling darkness; the evening star is shimmering behind the leaves of the fern tree.

I turn back to my roof terrace and sit sunk in my thoughts

until the light has swallowed the treetops and the cold has raised the hairs on my arms and legs. The sky is blue – like the lining of the Virgin Mary's cloak – and just as full of stars. Without putting on the light, I fumble my way along the wall of the spiral stairway down to my room. I lie down on the bed and pull the covers over me.

The window is open and there's a new moon. I know it will be a wakeful night and reach out for a scent from the garden, Passionaira, whose great leaves open in the breeze and act against insomnia. As long as I am awake, I can hope to keep my dreams at bay. Weeping Blood becomes the next name that comes to me from the Aztec herbarium, followed by Nightscent and Catclaw.

The whitish veil of the night mist creeps in over the sill and I lie as quite as a mouse. Then the mist is lit by a ray of moonlight and I sit up in bed.

I can hear a whinny from the wing with the empty stables. Maximilian's white Arab stallion flares through the darkness. Over a hundred years have evaporated like dew on a rose.

Wide awake and my mouth dry, I see the actors appearing on the last century stage.

From 'Oblivion' come footsteps, whispering voices from a servant whose bones have again turned to dust. Behind the French windows, candles are brought in, throwing reflections in the window-panes, and dishes of tropical fruits. Maximilian makes his entrance. For the occasion he has put on a silk shirt embroidered with the imperial monogram. Thoughtfully, he turns a diamond bracelet in its case of black velvet, and decants the wine.

He is waiting with excitement for La Conchita to finish her toilet. All through the siesta he has paraded at a rapid trot to her in his *Charro* costume – Mexican hat, embroidered velvet jacket, silver trouser seams, boots and spurs below. With flicks of his whip, he has demonstrated Vienna School dressage on the lawn, erect and with support against the pommel. From her basket chair on the terrace, she has followed him, more than once her gaze over the edge of her fan resting on his rider's thighs.

Soon she will appear to him in a negligée from one of the Paris fashion houses. La Conchita with her dark upward-curved lips and plunging hips, of which he intends to drink to the depths. He already feels the cloth of his trousers tightening, his tired blood flowing again. She has given him back his manhood.

Now she comes into the room from another room where he has long enjoyed the sound of her. She has made herself up to such an extent his lips twitch, though so discreetly she does not notice. The rouge on her high cheekbones is like a mask, the powder lumpy and her lipstick like something she has nibbled into her.

The line of her throat and the strong curve of her collar-bone make the lace and ruffles of her negligée droop. She smells of cinnamon, and clay that has stood out in the sun. He reaches for her. Again and again he empties the wine and plunges over her. She says nothing beneath the pressure of his loins, but the closed eyes quiver beneath the lids. . .

Not until morning when the light returns do their voices become a drone and gradually merge with the scent of the garden. It is the only cool time of day and it stings his eyes. Death's yellow flower and the Crania tree rule. I slide down under the covers and close the great book of the garden over my senses. I do not wake up again until far into the day, when the sun has beaten its way through the walls.

I abruptly sit up in bed and try to recall the events of the previous day.

3

The moment I open my eyes, I immediately know where I have seen the name Santos Linares before.

It was in Cuautla on a cross by the roadside.

The town is only an hour's drive away from here. I go into Cuernavaca, take the bus and we drive along the motorway. The old volcano looms on the horizon and beneath the mist, its belly, called the Snow-woman, slumbers for ever. Swirling clouds of dust dance across the plain and, from a distant point out there, a column of smoke curls its way up into the sky. I lean back in my seat and watch the details of the painting change as we roar through Morelos, the heat undulating beyond the windows.

I get off on the main road to Oaxaca. I have recognized an arena for bull-fighting and rodeo shows, and an eating place for truck drivers. A crossroads with some undergrowth and the edge of a ditch are the only signs I need to localize the place exactly. I search around for a while.

There, behind the billboard advertising Marlboro, the edge of the ditch comes in sight, the scrub with a silvery layer of road dust on its leaves. The midday light swings fiercely above and is thrown back from the turf like the singing of cicadas.

I root around at random with my foot in the scrub, striking in a circle until I come across a stone. One or two burrs have stuck to my trouser leg and as I bend down to pick them off, I see the cross appearing in my line of vision further ahead.

I straighten up. The cross is made of iron and is in a small concrete niche. At its foot lies a bunch of dead flowers. INRI is painted on the top. The name Santos Linares is inscribed on the crossbar in chalk-like handwriting. There is a date and on the back a year, 21 March 1978. Nothing else. Nothing but the day of death, leaving his birth in the unknown.

I am in a daze. At regular intervals a vehicle roars past, gears changing and horn sounding, but there is another dimension alongside this; petrol fumes and diesel drift down over an imaginary window. I search around in this world I have landed in and find a flower to put on his grave. Then I straighten up and brush the dust off my sleeves.

There is a row of booths on the opposite side of the road, selling refreshments. Tacos and tortillas, roast maize cobs and God knows what coloured liquids in plastic bags with straws protruding from them.

A figure has disengaged itself and is straying between the cars on the way across. Now and again it disappears in the heat haze or is occasionally obliterated by the cloud of a passing Pullman bus, but the figure grows – a leap closer each time. This is a four lane motorway. Fascinated, I follow the figure with my eyes. Again it is obliterated in a long drawn-out wail, then appears again on the other side of a passing line of trucks. Then at last it arrives on the edge of the motorway.

I see it is a woman as soon as it has become a body alongside mine, a woman in her early forties with grey streaks in her hair, an apron over her skirts and tortilla dough on her hands. She bends down and kisses the cross. When she straightens up again, a flower is lying beside mine, a yellow one.

We fall into conversation. I must have known the dead man as I have put a flower by his cross? It is clear she is also curious, her face turned questioningly towards me and an expression of disappointment spreading over it when I say no.

Now it's her turn to tell the story. He came early one morning in the year inscribed on the cross as a grim reminder. He got off the bus at the same place as I had and booked in at the motel opposite the arena. Every day he came to her booth, ate his tacos, his egg – always the same – and had a chat.

A shy friendship grew between them; he was as gentle as a child and the smallest thing aroused his wonder. He was slightly odd. He always called her Conchita, 'but my name's Estela', she added with a glance that still bears a light of grievance. Every day he seemed to forget what they had talked about the day before, and the same everyday things aroused his wonder yet again. The men reckoned he was not really all there.

At the time, Estela was married to Cuautla's handsomest bull-fighter, a wild youth on his way out of the slums, slightly younger than her. Manuel was his name and his love entailed watching jealously every movement she made. He did not allow any other man to come near her.

But he made an exception of Santos Linares. Santos was no threat: added to that his gaze was too distant. He remained a stranger there, mixing with no one, turning only to her. Rodeo cowboys regarded him as a kind of mascot, for that is what it's like with those who fall from the skies – they bring good luck. It was common for him to be there at their fights and performances. 'Come with us, Santito!' they always said – the little saint, the one who was more elevated than all the others. Manuel was indifferent.

None the less, it all went wrong. One day Santos came with a guitar he had acquired, a battered old thing with scratches on the varnish, but in his hands it sounded like a weeping child. He seemed to invent the notes from the start. Nor did anyone know the songs; perhaps they were his own, songs of oblivion, or of love – it is all the same to one who sings alone.

And lonely he was. When he played, it was heart-rending to listen to. The men wept and the women fell silent. The words remained obscure. It was poetry. Santos was a poet and gave the words a different meaning from what they had had before. But through all his verses ran the spectre of Conchita.

Estela began to understand why he always looked at her with his remarkably light eyes every time he came to the refrain. She was, as she said, a woman of flesh and blood. A secret serenade arose between them.

One evening when Manuel was in the arena, Santos came to her. He was more present than she had ever seen him, and also grandly dressed. Like a count. They stood in the moonlight and heard the voices roaring in the arena at every pirouette Manuel made with his sword and cloak before the bull. In that hour, Santos looked at her with a gaze that was freed of all else but the singing. She began to feel uncertain. She had not thought of their relationship in this light. He sang for her as he had never sung before and the songs were new. They were for Estela. For the first time, he used her proper name in his serenade.

The arena lay before them, bathed in its bright spotlights. The spectators in the little amphitheatre had risen to their feet in a collective roar of excitement. 'Kill it, kill it!'

She was frightened, and when Santos drew her to him to kiss her, she turned her head away. Her heart stood still in her breast and simply hurt. She did not know how she could say it. They had been so close. Suddenly she understood his loneliness, for when he came down to earth and was like everyone else it got between them like a pain and she knew at the same moment that she belonged to Manuel.

She pushed him away with great gentleness. She saw his gaze flee back into the shadows, raised her arms and took his head in her hands. 'Santos, Santos,' she whispered. But he was inconsolable.

At that moment a cry came from over by the gateway, which opened for the triumph of the toreador and cast a shaft of light over the scene. Manuel had come out, in high spirits and acclaimed, without his hat and with the bull's ear and tail in his hand. When he saw his beloved caressing another man, he threw down his trophies, thrust Estela aside and ran his toreador sword through Santos Linares's chest.

He fell face down. As they bent over him, they heard him groan:

'Men, I see you, you...'

His last words became air on his still-moving lips, then a spasm seized him, he rose on one elbow, saw the firefly swirl of the stars and gasped for breath. Then he collapsed and in his fall, crushed his guitar with a sound that penetrated to the very marrow. Out fell a photograph he had hidden in the bottom of the instrument. A photograph of the woman who had secured his unhappy soul, *un milagro*, Señor.

The men gathered around him in silence. Manuel was deathly pale, staring at the sword in his hand. Then he sank to his knees and gathered the dead man in his arms, but that made no difference. Their destinies had become interwoven, the living and the dead and equally lost.

Manuel watched over him for the rest of the night and the next morning he had gone. The authorities abandoned any further investigations into the case, writing it off as a road accident in line with the others on the roadside, and they raised a cross for Santos Linares on the spot.

'That's what happened, Señor. When I saw you, I thought perhaps you...'

She bites her tongue to stop herself pronouncing the tiny hope which has made her a widow of two men and bound her to a grief with no certainty. When I shake my head in silent pity, she jerks her head aside and mumbles an apology, then turns round and disappears into the glittering stream of cars.

Her image in the turbulent air drowns in reflections. I am again alone with thoughts I have pushed aside during her story.

I simply get on the next bus back to Cuernavaca. As we drive away, the afternoon light shimmers over the plateau. One side of the amphitheatre is brightly lit and the sun casts a long shadow over the spectator stands. It resembles – if you like – a sundial. Or a broken skull.

4

In Acapantzingo, the house is empty. I let myself in and allow the darkness to reign until dawn comes again. Not until the morning do I again go over to the garden, over to the cactus bed below the wall, then walk searching along the paths in this strangely laid-out desert, until I have found the prickly pear cactus on which Santos Linares has carved the letters of his name in triangular cuts.

Two dark blue butterflies in velvet costumes are fluttering around between the thorns. The date is covered with tissue and – I shrink inside – is the oldest in the garden. '1878' it says in childish handwriting. You can almost see the tongue in one corner of the mouth. I am not very numerate, but this cannot be right. The Santos Linares I have been told about is a man in his mid-thirties and not a centenarian.

It is not part of the official history, but there is much to indicate that Maximilian had a son by La Conchita. In 1878, he would have been a boy of about twelve.

During the First World War, a certain Count Sedano y Leguizano, which was Conchita's second name, appeared in France. That is what is known about him. He was said to be a direct descendant of the Emperor, whom that nation – more than any other – had left in the lurch. He threatened to visit Carlotta at Château Bouchout, where she was still wavering between light and darkness, draping the Empire's orders with rosettes, ribbons and veils over the back of her chair and carrying on long conversations with them during dinner, and where she refused to receive anyone. This presumably genuine descendant, but under any circumstances bogus count, was apparently wishing to ensure his heritage.

But it never got that far. On 10 October 1917, he was shot by the French who maintained that he was spying for the Germans. One thing can be said about that story – it doesn't hold water.

Carlotta died as late as 1927 – by which time she had shrunk to a little old woman of eighty-seven. Not until the last few years of her life was her incarceration in the gloomy castle over, and she was driven around the streets of Brussels in an open automobile with brass fittings and a rubber bulb horn. The photographs from the time indicate that she was at last at peace. They show a tiny little lady with a firm gaze beneath the cloche hat.

These dates and years confuse me with their fulcrums and dissonances. For if Santos Linares is identical with both the bogus count and the youth in the garden, how could he then die – first at the age of fifty – in the year of Our Lord 1917, and then again in 1978, still a youth at the age of a hundred and twelve? And if so, what is time?

Killing the man in Cuautla with a continuation of Maximilian's last words on his lips, and how many were to die before the sentence is completed?

I abandon guesswork and turn to the office to ask for *la doctora* of the previous day. Another shock. No one there has ever heard of her. The man who answers my questions is attached to the National Institute of Archaeology which runs the place and he regards me with a look of boundless scepticism. Did I get her name?

With rising confusion, I say I didn't. I must have been speaking to a lady from another period in time. That happens in a forgotten house when you enter by the back door.

To break the growing silence between us, he starts diverting me with details, really quite morbid, of Maximilian's embalming. He is otherwise a veterinary surgeon, fairish and with a beard, which is rare around here, but he is a thoroughbred Mexican when he talks about death. That is his Aztec heritage. Newspapers and magazines produce photographs every day of victims of road accidents and people who have been murdered, often close-ups so that you can see the cotton wool stuffed into the mouths and nostrils of the dead. In colour photographs they look strangely pop-eyed and their skin is bluish.

I feel sick and at once lose my desire to die in Mexico. The vet looks tight-lipped at me, speaking quietly, holding my eyes with a gaze that penetrates in under the eye sockets and bathes my insides in formalin vapour. So that there shall be no lie, I go to Chapulrepec Castle, where there is a photograph of the embalmed body.

I have meanwhile been in to see it.

Maximilian is lying with a raised bedhead behind him. His arms, hands and legs are wrapped in bandages, only there for the sake of the photo. They have no practical significance whatsoever. He has lost his lower jaw. There are large bare patches in his hair and beard. The glass eye bulges. On the faded and 'thinned' imprint of the photograph it is not possible to see whether it is open or closed. But the discolouring has already spread down his cheek.

Back to the vet, who has fallen into some indifferent thoughts that must stand on their own: Maximilian suffered from syphilis, which had reached an advanced stage, so he did not sleep with Carlotta. In retaliation, Carlotta became pregnant by one of his generals, Van der Smissen. That was her real reason for going to Europe. The insanity which then flared up was in reality due to an induced abortion! So we are quite up to date, and I hurry out of the house which no longer contains oblivion and rush home through the shadows of the garden.

I go up on to the roof terrace. It is an evening like any other in the area. The neighbour's dog is barking and a woman in the house opposite keeps calling in the same injured tones to her husband and children. She is standing in the light from the veranda room with a door out on to the swimming pool. Cars come up drives and doors slam. The cicadas have started up in the grass.

I lean out over the stone edge of the terrace. An inky black darkness has fallen over Maximilian's garden, a penetrating smell of camomile rising. I stand quite still, staring. For a long time. With a tense beating of my heart. Then there is a rustling in the leaves and a movement parts the foliage. Seen from up here it resembles a bridal veil. Who are you who lives for ever? I whisper after the figure disappearing among the trees – with cobweb-thin hands and hair gleaming in the moonlight.

THE NETHERLANDS

The Tree Saint

ATTE JONGSTRA

translated by Eric Dickens

...yea, they shall be afraid of that which is high, and terrors shall be in the way; and the almond tree shall blossom, and the grasshopper shall be a burden, and the caper-berry shall fail...
(Ecclesiastes 12:5)

The wrong question to begin with. But it's the one they often ask first.

'Why this tree?'

I sometimes compare it to the choice of school which city friends make for their child. Why should the child attend one specific school when there are other schools which are better? In ninety-nine cases out of a hundred they then go and say that the school simply happens to be the nearest one. And the teaching there isn't so bad after all, is it? Don't misunderstand me: I have nothing whatsoever to do with teaching. I am just not cut out to be an educationalist, even if simply for the reason that no one wants to listen to me. Not even the children. I really don't know why. I have sometimes thought that it is because my diction, the way I pronounce things, is different from the others. It can also have something to do with the fact that what I have to tell is too remote from the everyday experiences of most people.

I once asked a group of people listening to my sermon if they knew that the sun is a living organism, with a soul and so on. You should have seen their reactions! First sheer amazement, but that soon turned to hostility. They just simply couldn't cope with the thought. Too far from their kitchen gardens, and it was just as well that I gathered up my belongings and left in haste, it wouldn't have taken much more for the stones to start flying.

I am a far-sighted man and that puts fear into many a soul.

I can't say I haven't played on that fear. I did so quite consciously, I have to admit. But it was my mission, I could hardly have refused to carry it out. I was sent somewhere by the powers above because they hadn't got a grip on that part of the world any longer. To somewhere in the South of France. I wouldn't be able to point out the exact place on the map. Simply suppressed the memory, you could put it that way. What did I do there? Look, the Vatican once had someone burnt and I believe they regretted it afterwards. Afterwards... Two centuries later, if you don't mind!

Exactly. The Vatican has never exactly been over-hasty in admitting to feelings of remorse.

Nevertheless, the fellow they tied to the stake was very passionate in conjuring up distant visages, so fear-invoking that his audience was gripped with horror and fell to their knees, begging forgiveness. That can't have been particularly convenient for the Vatican at the time, I imagine; otherwise they wouldn't have gone and burnt him.

Then – afterwards – they again needed someone like that and their eye fell on me. For years, there had been rumours abroad that I saw things and expressed myself in a different manner from the way others saw things and expressed them: if they were only to give me suitable guidance, I would perhaps prove to be just the man to coax those thinking along inappropriate paths back into the fold of our Mother Church by way of my unusual vocabulary.

Talk about 'suitable guidance'! I was hedged in on all sides by various dignitaries... I don't know how this came about, but people tended to get lost again and again during my sermon. But I always managed to find them again. Nowadays, it seems to be quite the in thing to ask 'who is watching the watchers?', but in my case the answer is simple: I am.

When I returned, the Pope said with some surprise:

'Good Lord, your regular audience...You've still managed to keep them!'

'Yes,' I said. 'But it wasn't easy. And while I happen to be speaking to Your Holiness anyway, Your Holiness might do me the favour of giving me a quiet flock to tend, a small parish in the country. I am very weary.'

I saw him start on his purple cushions.

'Lord no,' he cried, 'that could lead to problems!'

'Oh I don't know,' I said. 'Among ordinary believers there is no one who listens to what I have to say. What did you imagine? That I preach to fish for fun?'

The Pope nodded. 'True, I suppose... That was you wasn't it?'

'That's what they say. I'd rather not be reminded of it. But I don't do much harm. Now tell me honestly...'

'Maybe you don't,' rejoined the Pope. 'But to say that I expect a great deal of good to come from you... That trip to France hasn't really helped a damn.'

The wages of the world is ingratitude, even in the world of the spirit. I had indeed preached in France until I was blue in the face. Surely, some form of reward could have been devised?

But to begin again at the beginning: when people ask why this tree...

I was not told by the Vatican which tree to take. Even that slight effort was too much for the Pope. I should arrange things myself, he told me. They could do little for me. In this instance, the word 'little' consisted of the limp handshake of a gloved hand and being escorted with undignified haste to the door. Period.

There I stood. I would have to start from scratch.

At such moments, a tree is perhaps not the worst of choices.

Does that sound odd?

This may be the appropriate moment to tell something about myself. About my earlier life. Nothing ever came of the monastery I once wanted to found in Morocco. I cannot deny that I have something of the missionary in me and I thought: Morocco is far enough away from Rome, there are probably opportunities there for a man like me. Clearly God thought otherwise. I became terribly sick and, convulsed by peristalsis, I returned with the very same ship. When I had recovered, I tried to fall into line with Rome once more. Well, so here I am again. Why did I have to attend that particular school? Why did I have to end up in a class taken by someone called Francis, a pauper? He talked to the birds, my fine mentor. Two-legged or four-legged, he would address everything and everyone as 'brother'.

'Can I help it that I've got a screw loose?' I even asked the Pope this. He merely shrugged his shoulders.

I did do a lot of reading. Francis had a private library. Not a large one. Most of the books were about ethnology or zoology. Habits and customs, subjects such as these. I remember reading in one of these books that many Greeks. . .

As an Italian you really get something out of such books! But you nevertheless manage to remember useless facts. You don't even know you've got them lurking in your head, but when they pop up you think: Damn it, that is something else I happen to know!

Many Greeks think that almonds. . .

Did I tell you that the tree I mentioned happened to be an almond tree?

'The almond,' the Greeks say, if I've got it right, 'is the Father of All Things.'

Every nation has its quirks. I could quite well imagine that another nation would have gone and chosen a cauliflower, a nation of fishermen would have picked an oyster, flower-growers a calyx so deep you could not see the pistil, woodcutters a huge oak tree, and so we have arrived back where we started. At a tree...

The almond is the first tree to bear blossom in the spring: that's no doubt where the idea arose. But to automatically assume that a woman is made with child by simply popping a sweet almond into her décolleté... What children they were, those Greeks! Francis also had an unshakeable belief in such tales. He believed everything that had been committed to writing. Innocence was writ large on his forehead. That's why people used to enjoy listening to him. The way he used to summarize things... To the point of naiveté; that appeals to any audience.

Christ Almighty!

'You're talking over the heads of the people, my lad...' Francis would often tell me.

I was always on the point of telling him that he should look to himself. He spent the whole day rambling on at birds, as if that wasn't talking over *their* heads. When I mentioned to him that I spent much more time than he did talking to my own species, he, of course, made that the crux of the matter.

'Keeping one's peace is an art, my son. If what you want to do is talk to people, then that is what they most like to hear.'

Holy smoke! What's all the fuss about? And you can take it from me that all Francis's aviary antics were merely a publicity stunt, though a pretty clever one, I can't deny. Look how famous they've made him. I'm still wet behind the ears in comparison. All doors were opened for him, including even the door of history. You often see him depicted in colour plates in books. Sometimes you only see birds, but everyone knows who's sitting amid them.

If birds land on my tree I can't help laughing out loud. 'Well, well, my dumb brethren!' I then cry out. 'So you thought that poultry had something to be gained here, eh? You can't just go cracking the nuts on my tree and get away with it just like that! There's more to it than that...'

They pretend not to understand me.

'You're even talking above the heads of the birds...'

Perhaps Francis did say that once, perhaps he didn't. But it is a saying typical of him.

Sometimes I shout something else. Something of the order of 'Have I got something of yours hanging on my tree? Have you lost something? Well, then I can tell you you've come to the wrong address!' That's the difference between Francis and me. He stood on the ground apostrophizing the birds, my vantage point is just that bit higher. I'm sitting in a tree, an almond tree. Why? I've got a simple answer to that one: so I can see a bit further without putting myself out. And I can say, furthermore: I happened to pick this particular tree, but any other tree would have done just as well.

An almond tree is by no means the worst, though the crown always looks a bit threadbare. In the right season it is full to bursting of nuts, mine is at any rate. I then move carefully through the branches and pick them all. At first I had to do quite a lot of acrobatics. It's thanks to my good luck rather than agility that I never fell down from the tree. Nowadays, I know how far I have to bend back the branches before they begin to creak, and I never lose my balance any more. That's what's good about it: if you keep it up for long enough, the very idea of falling simply doesn't occur to you any longer. I gather all the nuts into a basket which I have tied in the crook between two large branches. My larder.

Francis used to be happiest squatting down there among the people, I preferred to raise myself up a little. Not out of haughtiness I'll have you know, I am not making myself out to be any greater than I am. But simply to see something different from what everybody else sees, to enable me to tell people something new. Hence the tree. You see what I'm getting at?

Did you know that almonds are good for diarrhoea, periodontosis, acne, rheumatism, for insomnia and bad nerves? They are, furthermore, *the* remedy to counter palsy of the male member. And what is more: if you store up a supply of almonds you've always got something to nibble on. The mere idea that you've got something in your mouth is enough to dispel any pangs of hunger.

Last year I was sitting thinking of nothing in particular and peering out into the distance. I was enjoying the view, I do that quite often. Suddenly I heard a tinkly voice and saw a beautiful girl standing right under my tree. That is to say: she had a beautiful body but her face was full of spots and pock-marks.

'Can you really say that I'm such a beautiful girl?' she said. 'Breasts near the top of the alphabet like nobody else I know, belly as flat as a dining table and my bottom is two hemispheres. But look at my cheeks, full of scabs and lumps. Once I had skin like a peach: what ever happened to it?'

I suppose I managed to stammer something. Who was I to react to such things?

'I can see you're looking at me,' she said. 'Don't you believe me?' She immediately began unbuttoning her blouse.

'Whoa!' I cried. 'Stop that... In a minute I'll fall down next to you in the grass like a ripe apple!'

'Don't get so corny,' she said and looked up at me, wearily. 'Do you know anything for it, or don't you?'

Luckily she left it at that one button. I caught a glimpse of her cleavage. The chasm was deep enough as it was. Just to be on the safe side I clutched the branch on which I was sitting tightly and fixed my gaze on the horizon once more, beyond which the sun was just getting ready to set, in a flurry of flame. What could I say?

'Hello! Are you still there?' She sounded impatient.

'If you eat two almonds a day, every day, you will never suffer from skin blemishes, nor from things which lead to the malfunctions of the body. Once a week, after having got the functioning of your body nicely going by means of gymnastics, after having given all your limbs a good massage, you have to rub your whole body with almond oil. That keeps your liver and kidneys free from impurities.'

I didn't say anything else. She shouted something a couple more times. When I took a furtive glance down, I saw her sitting against the trunk. Later I took another look and she was gone. I have already mentioned the fact that I would rather not be reminded of the tales people tell about me, but that's how it is: as soon as you stick your head out above the rest of the field of waving corn they'll try to lop it off with the scythe of language. That may sound a little highfalutin', but it happens to be true.

The Vatican, for instance, has devised the word 'Saint' for this phenomenon.

Imagine you fall on the ice, end up in your sickbed and never appear to be likely to rise from it again. You get holes in your body the like of which medical men cannot find in any handbook, maggots crawl out of them, but nevertheless you manage to crack one witticism after the other: you can bet your life that there's a canonization waiting for you round the corner. Imagine that you have the sheer luck of being tied to a tree trunk and some myopic William Tell is let loose on you. The arrows piercing your torso and limbs are too numerous to be counted and since you have been so clumsy, so unusual as to not immediately lose consciousness – you even manage to make a wry little joke at the point where anyone else would long ago have given up the ghost – you get a sign round your neck with that word written on it.

'Saint'.

Imagine you have the bad luck to manage to levitate before all your bystanders are back home sitting round the table... before you know it they've gone and made you a 'Saint'. Anyone raising himself above the pack will get dragged down, back into the Church.

No wonder that the number 365 isn't large enough to give

each 'Saint' a birthday of their own!

Mine is the 13th of June. Falls on a very bad day. Can't even give people a plate of fresh almonds although they are the tastiest things in existence. Perhaps that's why no one ever comes to wish me a happy birthday.

Do I miss that? No, I'm past that kind of thing.

Tales, that's what I was telling you about. You should hear some of the things they say about me! That story about the fish was quite enough as it was... Who do people think I am? I'm also supposed to have performed a number of miracles. I'm supposed to have restored the leg of a child which its mother had hacked off because her little darling had given her a kick. I can't remember doing any such thing. I am supposed to have covered up a case of wife-beating by suppressing all traces of hæmorrhage. Managed to pass me quite unnoticed. An underfed mule is supposed to have sunk down on to its forelegs before my insignificant person out of sheer devotion while there was, *nota bene*, a sack right next to him bursting with oats. Which the creature didn't even offer a glance. Since when has Nature been like that? The wondrous resuscitation of a corpse, the raising of a sunken ship, influencing an infant to swear on oath, two fingers raised, that his mother had nothing to do with the adultery she was imputed to have committed?

Christ Almighty!

A year or so back, I heard a horse snuffling at the foot of my tree. I had not heard the creature approaching, I was, no doubt, sunk in thought. Not thinking about anything in particular, no doubt, simply sitting on the highest branch that would bear my weight and staring out towards the horizon: then you are as far away as you ever can be.

'*Hôla!* Sir... Brother!'

The rider was standing in the stirrups, as far as I could make out. A man in a brown habit. At that instant, I broke out into a sweat. He could very well be bringing me a message, and you could bet a thousand to one that the sender had his buttocks resting on purple cushions!

'*Hôla!* Would you be so kind as to come down from there?'

'Not a chance,' I cried. I was about to ask him what he wanted, but held my peace.

'I have come to get advice!' cried the knight.

'I see...' I said this as recalcitrantly as I possibly could. Advice... To someone in this uniform?

'What d'you think I'm sitting here in this tree for?' I asked. 'I don't have consultation hours...'

'None the less...'

There was something in his voice that betrayed it to be that of a determined man. When I secretly looked down, I could see that he had already dismounted, presumably firmly determined to give me no peace until he got what he wanted.

'This is the question,' he cried. 'The Pope has decreed that the Vatican City is to be expanded by the building of another suburb...'

'Which one?'

'What do you mean "which one"?'

'Whose arse at present rests upon the purple cushions?'

For a moment the man faltered, then he uttered a name that was unknown to me.

'I see,' I said. 'So *he*'s there nowadays...'

'That's right, but I've come to talk about the expansion. We're at the planning phase at present, His Holiness has expressed the wish for a daring, even a visionary, design. Something which has never before been carried out but would fit into the general pattern of present-day architecture. And considering the fact that you have made a study of Augustine as urban architect...'

'Augustine?' I cried, with as much surprise as I could muster. 'Who may that be?'

Stammering down by the trunk. 'Yes, well... I mean... And His Holiness had definitely said quite clearly that you...'

'The people say even more,' I said in a pleasant, level tone of voice which lay quite close to indifference. 'Will there be anything else?'

'Well, not really... That was more or less my message.'

'*Bene*,' I cried with relief. 'Greetings to His Holiness! *Pax vobiscum!*'

Such turns in the conversation always give a certain measure of relief, especially if they are followed shortly afterwards by the sound of horses' hooves fading away. Relief followed by resentment when you notice that in the broad landscape of your peace of mind that knight still stands in his stirrups with his untoward questions. Naturally I knew who Augustine was. But right from the very start, I have tried, in my tree, to forget those I have wished to emulate. Indeed I wished to empty my head of everything. If it was to be so, I must have thought at the time, that if, because of the Pope, I would have to forego a quiet parish in the country, then it would be best to forget all about pastoral duties altogether. In that case it is better not to think of other pastors, certainly not of someone such as Augustine. If you wish to start afresh, then it is vital to eliminate old mentors. It was a good thing that they existed, they have brought you to the point you are at now, and there will certainly be plenty of their words left lurking somewhere inside your head, but they mustn't begin to weigh too heavily on your everyday cogitations. Then everything becomes... Well, everything then grows very thin.

Except for the Father of All Things; Him I cannot simply remove from my mind. It is perhaps a peculiar expression, it has something almost Greek about it if you know what I mean, but that's how I see it none the less: every day I sit right in the middle of Him.

I have already mentioned the fact that there are many stories abroad about me, about the period before I took up residence here. Since then, only one has been added, a fable which is rather self-evident. Quite inaccurate, but nevertheless understandable, is the nickname I seem to have acquired of late. How do I know? On occasions, children stray further from home than their parents would wish and standing under my tree, jeer and call me 'Anthony the Stylite!' What a plague. Mostly, I ignore them. They're children, after all. On rare occasions I cannot stand it any longer. If I'm in luck and the almonds are ripe then I shake a branch. Nuts rain down and they are soon gone, those nasty urchins. Standing out of reach they carry on annoying me, but soon get fed up.

Once a car stopped. A modern contraption with four-wheel drive. Terrain vehicles I believe they are called. On the sides of the vehicle something was written. If I remember rightly the text said the 'Guinness Book of. . .' something or other. A fellow got out and asked me in pidgin Italian how long I had been sitting here.

'Centuries!' I cried. 'What's it to you?'

'That depends on you,' he said. 'If you have no objections to being listed under "stylites", then there's a good chance of your getting an entry!'

'For heavens' sake keep me out of the books. There are enough rumours about me doing the rounds as it is!'

I should like to put it this way: to keep history unsullied, you have to give some writers the cold shoulder.

Periods occur where a particular story, the interpretation of events or a historical figure suddenly prove to be very popular. Perhaps it is like it is with jokes. You don't hear them for years and suddenly everyone is telling each other the same one. 'Do you know the one about that fellow who sits in a tree and retrieves everything you've lost?'

That fellow in the tree. Perhaps the strength of such jokes lies in the 'that'. I term that word 'the indeterminate allusion', an expression of which I am rather fond. And yet I hate jokes, but that's not the point right here. And you could ask yourself whether the joke about the 'fellow in the tree' was really that funny. I have evidence to the contrary.

I have difficulty in remembering the exact occasion on which I saw the first object flying at me. I had been sitting a good while in my tree, and my sense of time had left me long ago. There had been days and nights, more than just a few. But I never thought of counting them. It was a bunch of keys, I remember that quite clearly, and soaking wet. It glittered in the sunlight. And when it flew in a little arc over my head I felt a couple of droplets in my neck. I can also recall a light chinking sound as it fell in the grass. I looked in astonishment at the keys fastened to the large ring, turned my gaze to the horizon as I always do when some thinking has to be done, looked again at the bunch of keys and got an unpleasant feeling. No lock in sight, right in the midst of nature, and then that bunch of keys. What could it mean? What can you do if there are no further signs? Other marvellous things occur, and if no pattern establishes itself within a given time then you forget them. They vanish, as it were, under the grass in your head, they become overgrown, and that is in fact what happened here. Some while later, a goat suddenly appeared in my field of vision. The creature started bleating like nobody's business and looked rather lost, but managed to end up on all fours and began grazing as if it belonged here. Only then did I remember the bunch of keys, but I could not with the best will in the world see any connection between them, and paid no further attention to the goat and the keys.

I have sometimes asked myself why the figure three is so hypnotic a figure. Even as far back as in the Bible. I never did find an answer. Many explanations have, of course, been put forward. I remember a number of these from Francis's private library. They didn't mean much to me. I just know that I began asking myself what all these flying objects in my field of vision were doing, especially when a bicycle appeared complete with plastic carrier bag with empty bottles which chinked against one another.

What can be the link between a bunch of keys, a goat and a bicycle, I thought to myself. An enigma, in the jaunty spirit of 'What's the difference between a dead bird? One of its legs is as long as the other.'

Please forgive me. You get a bit daft sitting there alone in a tree for so long. Inexplicable occurrences also make you a shade too jolly on occasions.

So that you can laugh away your dread, put it that way.

But that laughter died in me. A period broke out where the air was full of random objects such as a purse, a cat or dog, a scarf, a letter, a suitcase. . .Objects, in other words, which people lose. After a while, the ground around my tree was strewn with them. There were things lying all over the place, even severed arms, legs, dead lovers, et cetera.

'I can see that it's not all over yet,' I muttered to myself, softly, when I looked out over the chaos. 'Soon it'll be summer and they'll start going off, with all the stench that involves.' That will have been when I began hearing voices.

My name was called out, first in connection with a bunch of keys which was supposed to have fallen out of a breast pocket into a canal:

'Oh St Anthony, I've lost my keys. Can you find them for me, heavenly rider, please.'

What can I say? It rhymed. Well, what did you expect? That bunch of keys was only the beginning. I would have been crazy if I'd started retrieving all those lost objects. The goat I could perhaps have given a good crack across the withers. Half way across the field the creature would perhaps pick up the scent of home, you never know. But I would have had to get down from my tree to do that. And that was not the idea.

The result of this turn of events was that my beloved almond tree became the centrepiece, first of a large open-air junk shop, later of a huge rubbish tip. I saw more and more people turning up. Whether they found what they had come for, I do not know, but no one went home empty-handed. I even saw someone fall to his knees and make the sign of the cross. I interpreted that as intended for me. Later on, I was treated like a showman to whom you can give a piece of your mind, however loudly I used to cry that I had nothing to do with my surroundings.

'We've heard differently,' people would then say.

Those damned tales!

The next turn of events was that people began slinging things in my face such as 'pickpocket' and 'magpie'. I even heard 'groper of hens'.

Christ Almighty!

'Because the tales, this grapevine publicity, can bring you to the point where you retreat from the world up a tree. That, after a time, you look around you and see what it has become... Did you know that the almond tree is part of the rose family? Because you rediscover yourself, literally, as a rubbish tip rose, amid people who are all dissatisfied, looking for something they have gone and lost... Because there has to be someone, perhaps because of a vision which is, after all, that bit higher...'

I'm not really sure whether this is the right way to open a speech, but that's what I heard myself saying. The reactions were none too promising. I didn't look up: it had never been any different. People carried on rooting around in the rubbish strewn around me. Here and there people would fight for lost objects lying around which everyone claimed as theirs.

'Ladies and gentlemen!' I now cried. 'May I have your attention for a moment? There are rumours circulating about me which I would like to dispel...'

Loud yelling. I didn't understand much of what was going on. Under my tree stood a giant of a man, with a voice that befitted his stature. He shook a bunch of keys, said they were his, but that I had appropriated them. He would like to know what I had to say about this.

I looked down in surprise at his luxuriant shock of hair. I hardly thought him the type to want to listen to the other side of the argument. But I had to make the most of the opportunity, and everyone suddenly fell silent.

'Ladies and gentlemen! The tales people are telling about me are untrue and I should like to prove this.'

The giant had clearly decided it was time for his reply to be heard: 'That object is standing there in the midst of lost property, in a tree in which everyone thinks he should stay, and has the effrontery to claim that it's all a myth. Reality has caught up with you!'

For just a moment I'd lost the thread. 'Give me some petrol, give me a lighter!' I cried. 'And I'll show you what'll remain of your legend.'

I believe there to be moments in the life of a man when, driven to the utmost, you want to prove that there are things which are beyond your powers. As I say this, I now realize that people who have matched their words with deeds often end up in the catalogue of saints. The Vatican obviously has a nose for such things.

'Give me some petrol, give me a lighter,' I shouted once again. The man under the tree looked hesitantly upwards: 'Do you think it's a good idea to go through with it, old fellow?'

I couldn't be stopped now.

'Give me. . .' I began again, but they handed me a jerrycan. I stretched a long way down, grabbed it, unscrewed the top and tipped the contents over my head. Whereupon a lighter that somebody had found was most obligingly produced and thrown up to me.

'You're getting what you asked for,' I shouted.

The three women who were busy knitting, sitting on a pile of suitcases in the front row, nodded and called in unison that they considered it a good thing that they had not come for nothing, since they hadn't been able to find anything that they recognized as theirs on the whole damned tip.

'You're looking too near to home,' I said. 'Distant faces, that's what it's all about. Ladies and gentlemen!'

With my thumb I pressed the knob of the lighter, a second movement of my thumb produced a light. A few seconds later I stood uplifted above the searchers like a lighted beacon in tongues of flame. Then the basket of almonds also caught fire – I must have spilt some of the petrol – and I imagine the whole tree burst into flame. One notch above all those people, all those things you manage to remember quite well once you've found them again.

I stood there like. . .

Now that I can see my story in context, I have to admit that a number of elements in it have adopted the character of what you tend to find in the lives of saints. Including this: the fact that I can tell what happened, that I've managed to keep the story in my head and even retrieve it at the appropriate moment. . . I say this in all humility, but perhaps this is the best proof that I have managed to ease my way up that bit higher and see just that little bit further than lesser mortals.

ITALY

Something Red

PAOLA CAPRIOLO

translated by Liz Heron

Once, in a wooded region, remote from all the well travelled roads, there rose a great windowless building that was painted a greyish colour which was sometimes tinged with green, and sometimes blue; only a narrow little gateway, its double doors grey too and almost always closed, unobtrusively broke the utter uniformity of this exterior. Despite appearances, the building was no prison, but the abode of a group of men of every age and social rank who had chosen to live together in accordance with strictly established rules. Young and old, rich and poor, all were united by a deep repugnance for that which in human life is random and ephemeral, and for their very own being, random and ephemeral in itself. On entering this community each of them had shed his own name, and if he was called Tizio or Caio his fellows would address him as 'Non-Tizio' or 'Non-Caio', or else if he was fair he became known as 'Darklocks', if he was thin 'Fatman', in such a way as to be simultaneously one thing and also its opposite, which, in the unanimous judgement of the confrères, represented unquestionable progress on the way of perfection.

Among these men there was one so young that they had re-baptized him 'Whitelocks'. He had already been there for some time, but no one could have said how long, since in that community it was severely forbidden to keep account of the months and the years, or in any way to devote attention to an entity as absurd, outrageous and patently non-existent as time. Thus only the shifting of the light, which fell from a sheet of glass on the roof of the building to shine faintly upon its windowless rooms, measured the slow days of Whitelocks, and by degrees he accustomed his eyes to make no distinction between this weak glimmer and that which was cast by the night hours. In the same way he accustomed himself to disregard the taste of food, to have no preference for one over others of the confrères, and never to fix his thoughts on any one particular thing, in order that he might embrace the formless totality in which, according to the teachings of the elders, all particular things should merge and be obliterated. Towards this totality, this nothingness, his desire was impelled with growing fervour, and in its name the young man regarded his own self with irritation, or at most forbearance, and it seemed to him that he inhabited his person as if it were some prison which, in keeping him separate, held him apart by force from that single, true reality.

This feeling gripped him so strongly that he greeted neither with joy nor with fear the news that, having now surmounted the initial period of complete seclusion, he too would sometimes have to venture out of his retreat; indeed it was usual that after every full moon it would fall to three of the confrères to betake themselves to the nearest city, or rather to the one least distant, to collect the alms bestowed on them by rich benefactors.

On the eve of the day established for Whitelocks's first sortie, Infant, the deacon of the community, summoned him to his room. 'Are you certain it is not too soon?' he asked him. 'If you are not yet so inclined, you may refuse.'

'Why should I not be so inclined? Believe me, the idea of seeing the world again does not move me in the slightest.'

'Be mindful though that you must enter sumptuous palaces, and visit persons whose life seems rather enviable to many.'

'Not to me.'

'And the city itself, so beautiful as to compel whoever sets foot in it to wonderment, and the women whom you will certainly encounter in the streets...'

'Nothing of all this can trouble me.'

'Since it is so, we shall go together tomorrow morning: not-you, not-I and our confrère Chatterbox.'

The next day, at dawn's first light, the three therefore set out. With detachment Whitelocks observed the disc of the sun climb above the horizon and insinuate its ever brighter rays into the gloomy shadow of the trees; a mendacious light, he thought, a cruel light which imprisons things in sharp contours and presents to our eyes a fir tree with long curved branches, a thicket of brushwood, the faded splendour of a rosebed, presents all these evanescent images as if they had real solidity, and ensnares the unschooled spirit in the woeful illusion of the world. Upon him, he noted with pride, images like this exercised no charm, and so, in the footsteps of the confrères, he crossed woods and meadows, hills and plains, as if between him and what he saw there rose still the high grey walls of his retreat.

Nor did this indifference diminish in the city; the masterly perspectives, the limpid harmony of the squares spoke to him in a foreign language, and sometimes when crossing the path of a woman he would perceive her beauty with cold dispassion, but he did not even turn, and would go on his way serenely holding the quizzical gaze of the deacon. In the splendour of the palaces he felt neither envy nor awe; he ate and drank from precious dishes as if it were a matter of his wooden bowl, and thanked without gratitude whoever offered him alms, since, as he had been taught, gratitude too is a danger, it sways the spirit from the all, while the benefactor should be loved no more nor less than the enemy or than oneself, or none of the three of them loved, or better still, the very distinction between love and not loving expunged resolutely from the heart.

It was already afternoon when they took the way back. Whitelocks walked quickly ahead of the confrères, anticipating the sense of triumph with which he would close the grey doors of the gateway behind him and tell himself that he had visited the world and returned from it without the slightest alteration taking place within him. Beneath his unshod feet the road became a path which, ever more winding, left inhabited areas behind to bury itself in the woods. This solitude provoked intense relief in the young man, seeming to him a slow approximation of the absolute calm which he would soon enjoy once more.

Suddenly an uproar wrenched him from his reflections; shouting, barking, and a riotous commotion which seemed to issue from the dark depths of the wood. Whitelocks stopped without thinking. 'What is going on?' he asked Infant. 'What can this noise be?'

'What does it matter?' replied the old man with an indulgent smile. 'It is a noise like so many, a fragile little thing made of air which is born somewhere, knows its brief life and is spent, almost so as to depict, with allegorical clarity, the vanity of this world of ours...'

But Whitelocks was not listening to the deacon's teachings; he stared at the path then quickly turned his eyes towards a thicket that was suddenly alive with a screeching sound.

'What is the matter with you?' said Infant, noticing his preoccupation.

'Didn't you see? An injured fox. It crossed the path and hid among that brushwood.'

'Yes, I thought I noticed something red, there in front of us, but of course I paid no heed.'

'Nor I,' said the third confrère, 'I was too absorbed in listening to Infant's wise words.'

'It was limping, hardly able to move, and yet trying to run.

It turned to look at me for a moment, with such fearful eyes...'

'Oh, really?' said Infant. 'Well, this gives an answer to your question just now: the noise we heard was evidently made by a group of hunters, and the fox is their prey. But it would seem that it has managed to elude pursuit, since the noise, if you attend to it, is getting further away in the other direction. Now, assuming you have no objection, I should like to continue on the way; we have already stopped too long for so pointless a reason.'

Whitelocks obeyed, yet all along the now short road that separated them from their goal he could not help but turn at every least squeak of sound to explore with his eyes the tangled thickness of the vegetation. He did it furtively, almost as if he wished to conceal his anxious seeking not just from his fellows, but even from himself, and he experienced an unfamiliar feeling which his thoughts condemned and yet were incapable of casting out.

'What is a fox, after all?' he kept saying to himself. 'It is the same thing as a horse, or a gull, or a man: a nothing, a fleeting reflex destined soon to disappear. I know this, and I knew it before; so what difference can be made by the fact that I have seen that injured fox, that one creature among a thousand others who suffer and die every day?' None, replied his reasoning; an infinite difference, another voice came back in answer, ever stronger and insistent. Observing it on the path he had caught only a confused glimpse of the animal, so brief had been his sight of it, but the limping gait, the desperation of its attempts to run, the terror and the suffering that its gaze expressed, had become deeply etched in his memory, tormenting him without respite. That pain, those eyes, that injured paw seemed to him to belong to the fox like a property unto it alone, so as to transform it into a unique and unmistakable creature, a creature to whom Whitelocks, however hard he tried, could not manage to attach names such as 'non-fox' or 'the joyful one', in accordance with the wise baptismal rules he had learned from the confrères.

The sun was setting when they arrived back at the building, whose walls in that terminal glow took on a purplish tinge. His companions turned towards the refectory, but Whitelocks did not wish to follow them, feeling that he would not be able to eat.

'Yes,' said Infant, 'it is better for you to go to bed at once. You are very pale, the road must have tired you.'

As soon as he was in his room Whitelocks undressed and stretched out on his straw mattress. Staring at the bare walls, he continued to see before him the path and the fox staggering across it on three paws. 'Something red,' the deacon had said, and he tried still to persuade himself that this was all he had seen, a simple image bereft of reality, like everything which is entrusted to time and destruction. But for the first time he was unable to believe that pain had no reality; he could not, because it was suffering itself which seemed to confer on that fox an incontrovertible being. The contorted paw and the eyes dilated in terror urged themselves upon him like an absolute truth which no reasoning could ever shrink to mere appearances. There was no doubt that the wound bled, with real blood, appallingly substantial, and in a flash the idea that this blood could in any way be redeemed by the pale, remote totality to which he and the confrères addressed their cold devotion appeared absurd to him. There was no calm, no supreme reconciliation which had the means to cancel out that pain, to deny its meaning; if he had always regarded time as an unceasing dissolution in which each instant vanished without leaving any trace, the moment when he had seen the injured fox denied this belief and clung on firmly to his memory and compassion.

In the grey building everyone slumbered, but Whitelocks could not fall asleep. At last he could resist no longer; he got up, dressed, took a blanket and, taking care not to be heard, he reached the entrance gate, guided by the flickering light of a lamp. He took down the key which hung from a heavy nail on the wall, turned it in the lock, and, once he was outside, closed both halves of the door behind him with the utmost care. Before him he saw the wood, into whose darkness the full moon shone gleams of silver. 'Whatever has entered my mind?' he thought. 'I must be mad.' Yet he did not turn back; holding the lamp aloft he set forth on the path and continued until he found the place where he had caught sight of the fox. He recognized the thicket into which the animal had disappeared, and entered it. Then he proceeded almost on all fours, groping along the ground with his free hand, and could not but let out a cry of joy when all at once he felt beneath his fingers a soft coat of fur which rose and fell to the rhythm of laboured breathing. But then he thought that the fox must have been gravely injured, since it had not fled on hearing his approach, and his good humour vanished.

He lifted it with care and wrapped it in the blanket. The fox, inert like some lifeless thing, made no protest, only turning its head slightly towards him and staring at him for a moment with a timorous, questioning look. Whitelocks was tempted to caress it, but a certain reserve prevented him from performing an action so at variance with how he was accustomed. Carrying the bundle with great difficulty he hurried back to the grey building and was able to re-enter his room before the confrères woke. Here he laid the fox on the pallet, released it from the blanket and examined it. Already, the blood had ceased to flow from the injured paw. 'You will heal, but you would have died of hunger or been devoured by some bigger creature had I left you in the wood in these conditions.' He lay down beside it, and at last succeeded in falling asleep.

In the following days several members of the community observed that the young Whitelocks was spending more time than usual in his room and often took his full bowl with him there. They noticed besides that some rolls of gauze and a whole pot of ointment had disappeared from the infirmary. Very soon all of this was reported to the deacon, who took it upon himself to make a personal enquiry into the causes of the strange behaviour; he therefore waited for a day when it was Whitelocks's turn to be on duty in the kitchen in order to enter his room by stealth, but to his great amazement he found the door was locked. 'For this too,' he thought, 'he will have to account to me.'

Towards evening, when he returned after finishing his work, Whitelocks saw Infant in front of the door. The deacon eyed him with a stern suspicious look and his gaze lingered for some moments on the brimming bowl of food scraps which the young man held in his hand.

'Welcome back, Whitelocks.'

'Have you been waiting for me for a while? Tell me what you want.'

'I want nothing, only madmen want. But I must speak to you; this is why I have waited for you.'

'I will join you shortly in your room.'

'Why do you not have me enter yours instead?'

Whitelocks lowered his head without answering.

'And since when,' Infant went on, 'have you become accustomed to locking your door?'

'I did not know it was forbidden.'

'It is not, in fact.'

'In which case. . .'

'But no one uses his key, unless he should have something to hide.'

'I am hiding nothing.'

'All the better. Then you will not mind allowing me to enter.'

Resigned, Whitelocks opened up and made way for the aged confrère. Hearing the key in the lock the fox had approached the door, but on seeing a stranger in front of it, ran to take cover beneath a piece of furniture.

The deacon said nothing; he sat down on the straw mattress and with a solemn movement of his hand ordered the young man to do the same. 'Yes,' he murmured at last, 'now I remember. Now I understand.'

'I am happy that you understand.'

'Don't mistake my meaning, Whitelocks; recognizing the reason for an action is not the same as justifying it, and I cannot justify your error, your blindness.'

'The animal was injured, you know this too.'

'And what of that?'

'It would have died, if I had not looked after it.'

'And what of that? It will die however, sooner or later.'

'But not now, and not from my doing.'

Infant shrugged his shoulders. 'From your doing? It was not you who injured it. You had no duty towards that beast, you should have thought of its fate with the same detachment with which you think of yours, mine or that of any other creature.'

'I well know how I should have behaved, according to our principles...'

'Why do you say: "our principles"? From the moment when you choose not to follow them, do not assume them as your own. No, Whitelocks, you are not worthy of resting in the sacred calm of the Whole.'

'Perhaps you are right.'

'You drew your eyes away from it to turn them to the particular, you let yourself be caught in the treacherous snares of pity. To reject the world you must be able to expunge compassion too.'

Emboldened by the presence of Whitelocks, the fox had left its hiding place and had approached the bowl. 'Yes, it is as you say,' the young man murmured as he watched it eat. 'I belong to the world now, not to this place.'

The deacon was silent for a long while, and when he spoke

again his tone was more indulgent. 'Come now, do not despair; you can still repent and repudiate your error. The community is prepared to forget what has happened provided that you undertake to observe the rules with scrupulousness in the future.'

'What must I do?'

'You know very well.'

The fox had emptied the bowl down to the last mouthful and now curled up in a corner. It had one paw tucked under its body, the other, the one wrapped in gauze, stretched out on the floor.

'I cannot let it go, it isn't able to survive alone. As soon as it has recovered...'

'I could permit you to keep the animal, if you were to regard the thing with the necessary indifference. But it is no matter of indifference to you whether this creature stays or goes away, and this is precisely what is wrong. Examine your feelings and tell me if it is not so.'

'It is indeed so. I am not indifferent to whether it lives or dies.'

The deacon rose. 'There is nothing left to be said, it seems.'

'I shall leave tomorrow morning: the time to gather my things...'

Infant gave his silent assent and walked slowly from the room. Alone now, the young man approached the fox. 'What do you think, have I gone mad? I have renounced calm and wisdom, I have renounced my highest hopes, and in exchange I will have only cares and disappointments, joys that do not last.'

The fox stared at him. Whitelocks stretched out a hand, laid it on its back, and for the first time, with a tentative movement, caressed it. He thought of the next morning when, carrying his bundle and the fox wrapped in the blanket, he would pass through the little gateway while the confrères still slept, and would turn from the path to cast one final look at the high grey walls. Then the forest would greet him, with its alternating light and shade, its thousand-fold forms, the heat of all the ephemeral lives which found shelter within it. It would give him shelter too, in some cave, in some cabin or in one of the many villages scattered along its edges; in one way or another he would obtain enough food for himself and the fox and would go on taking care of it, until the time came to set it free again. Then he did not know what would happen. He had aspired to raise himself above the towering affairs of the universe, and now he could not imagine himself without that small animal with the bandaged paw. He took the fox in his arms, stretched out with it held beside him, and little by little he fell asleep; and each time he felt its breath stir lightly on his face he experienced a great fear and a strange, intense happiness.

PORTUGAL

The Journey

NUNO JÚDICE

translated by Margaret Jull Costa

1

When he got into the carriage, he found himself in the midst of an indescribable jumble of people: peasants in muddy boots lying stretched out on seats, their legs or heads resting on vast wicker baskets; soldiers in need of a shave yelling obscenities at each other, their greasy hair sticking out like clumps of damp grass from beneath their caps; children bundled into jackets several sizes too big for them, cheap fur collars hiding their faces; bags blocking the narrow corridor; old women speaking in southern dialects, discussing prices and land; a few civil servants struggling to maintain an appearance of dignity, quite superfluous in the circumstances, nervously clutching the silver buttons on their overcoats and staring out of the misted windows, through which you could just make out the blurred contours of square, anonymous buildings.

The warehouses of the Empire, he thought, every one crammed, in as disorderly a fashion as its subjects on the train, with the detritus of lives repeated over successive generations, warehouses that the storm winds of History had now demolished as thoroughly as any earthquake, to reveal at last the decaying foundations. How much of all this – people and merchandise – would be condemned to rot there, transforming those provincial railway stations into great becalmed cargo ships slowly eaten away by the sea until all that's left are carcases corroded by salt, rust glinting palely in the brief autumn dawns, waiting for the winter storms to send them to the bottom for good?

He managed to get a seat by the window. His gaze fixed on the ceiling, blackened by the smoke and dust of many journeys but still bearing traces of gold paint. He could feel himself drifting off into sleep, yet he remained in a state of wakefulness that the hours of immobility, waiting for someone somewhere to give the signal for them to leave, had transmuted into a torpor warmed by prolonged contact with the tangle of bodies.

He woke up suddenly in the middle of the night. A heavy silence reigned in the compartment.

The other people were all asleep, arranged in the most extraordinary positions. In one corner, you could hear a woman's intermittent sobbing, but her identity remained cloaked in darkness. His legs felt heavy from the long hours of not moving, but he didn't dare get up for fear of antagonizing the carriage's slumbering belly. He became aware of the sound of rain beating on the window. The noise grew louder as the rain grew heavier, provoking hurried footsteps along the platform, which, with the lighting of the swaying lamps, sprang to hallucinatory life. Now there was movement inside the compartment too: people torn from sleep wiped at the windows, trying to peer out through the rain into the darkness. Beneath the noise of rain and shifting humanity he thought he could hear an almost imperceptible panting.

A child began to cry and, moments later, a sudden shuddering startled the whole ghostly universe properly awake: the train was on the move. The men sat up in their seats, then got to their feet, yawning and stretching. A hoarse whistle pierced the night, the sound lasting beyond the initial exhalation that was gradually quickening to become the obsessive rattle of the carriages, stirring into activity lives which, for hours now, had been held in abeyance.

2

The speed slackened. He'd allowed himself to fall asleep and was now being shaken awake by the man next to him. 'I think we're going to stop.' He glanced out of the window. The sky had the whitish tone of childhood mornings. In the winter, he used to go out into the garden at dawn and stare across at the horizon on the far edge of the plain which, at that hour, looked like a frozen sea. A stiff breeze would be blowing, heavy with salt and silence, and he would simply let the images fill his head until his body was too cold to bear it any longer. Sometimes it rained. It was a penetrating rain that drenched him to the soul. Then, everything would stop. He could hear the horizon: a legacy from the depths of memory. He would stand for hours waiting for the sky to fall. No one would speak to him. They would gather around him, as if to pray, and he was aware of their faces and their half-closed eyes, the slow movements of their lips, the linen scarves the old women wore about their heads. By then the evening wind would be blowing in from the plain and still they would all be standing there, as if performing some strange act of penance.

He'd left them in that position and now he found them again, after all these years, gathered around him exactly as he'd left them, this time in the guise of passengers on a train that was slowly drawing to a halt. He stretched out his fingers towards them but touched only the air thick with the acrid smell of bodies and tobacco.

'I think we're going to stop.'

The voice wakes him. The carriage doors open, letting in a blast of icy air. One section of the compartment empties of passengers. People are running across the frozen earth alongside the carriages. Shouts are heard that echo against the sky, causing little flurries of snow to fall, covering the trees lined up along what he assumed to be a river. The carriages of the train are lined up too, like a wall that had sprung up out of nowhere, the engine still wheezing at the front, but keeping to a gentler rhythm now. Various explanations for the stop are put forward: the line is blocked, a bridge is down.

A strident whistle is the signal for renewed movement. People rush to the train doors. The snow is stained with footsteps, the mud showing through here and there. And everything begins again, the grubby damp of the seats mingling with the indifference brought on by weariness. Then the noise changes, the rattling of the carriages alters as they pass the arches of a bridge that sway in sequence outside the window. It's pointless trying to see out: a thick fog descends as the sun sets. Chunks of black bread are handed round. The soldiers finish off a bottle of brandy. They start trading obscenities again, but it seems that now even they do not hear them. The hours of prolonged indolence infect ears and brain alike. Life itself disappears along with the landscape devoured by the night.

3

He was on a stationary train in the middle of the night, not sure whether he was asleep or awake. He couldn't leave. Besides, he had no way of knowing if the train would start moving again.

The train was standing in a station identical to many others it had passed through on this journey. Perhaps that's why it was a matter of indifference to him whether he got out or stayed, not that anyone was keeping him there. He was free to leave everything behind him, to cross the deserted station platform, walk to the nearest village and sit down on a bench.

Perhaps he'd fallen asleep again. Behind him he could hear the noise of wings beating and the noise began to trouble him. It was a kind of shadow, a sound-shadow. 'Have you ever wondered what it would be like if your shadow made a noise?' he said to the man sitting opposite him. 'After a while, you'd be afraid to move even a finger, or else you'd try to rid yourself of your shadow altogether by living in total darkness.' Perhaps that was what his shadow wanted, for him to melt into it, for him to hand his own life over to it. And the truth is that he could actually feel himself becoming a shadow. And the shadow stepped away from him, walked over to the station forecourt and into the square on the other side of the building, where everything was closed and silent.

It had started to snow again. He went over to the fountain in the middle of the square. There's usually a statue in the middle of the fountain: a king, an emperor, a saint or a god, but always a strangely human god. He broke the ice covering the water in the fountain and plunged his hand in. It was warm. Yes, with his hands in the water he could feel the divine warmth. Inside himself, however, there was utter solitude. Emptiness. Ice. He could hear nothing apart from an occasional muffled murmur coming from the houses: the wind moaning in the timbers.

And then the engine screeches into life again. He runs to the carriage, tripping over boxes piled along the platform. He enters the compartment: and there he is! He'd forgotten that it was his shadow that had gone outside. He was just an inert body, stretched out among all the others just like him, prisoners on a pointless journey.

He sits up again. 'The birds,' he says. Yes, one winter night, he'd gone to the village. An old man was drinking brandy. From time to time, he'd lean on the balcony and talk, laughing to himself: 'That was when I heard the birds. It happened quite suddenly, I think. They all began to sing at once. The lights went on in the houses; women came to the windows. No one had ever heard music like it. It was as if a comet had flown across the whole of space, carrying with it a divine song, and come to a halt immediately above me, together with its entourage of fire. The birds came from all over, they burst out of the earth, they filled the air. And the birds were made out of light. It was an incredible night. And then it stopped, as suddenly as it had begun. Absolute silence.'

Then, once again, the train reverberates to the clink of metal, the noise of wheels on tracks, drunken laughter. He asked the old man what he was laughing about. 'Death brushed past me and touched me with his scythe,' he said.

The man was laughing at his own death!

4

He'd finally fallen asleep. He was walking among the trees. The leaves, hardened by frost, cut him like blades. His body left a trail of blood in the snow. He could even feel the breath of wolves on his hands. He fell and the snowflakes covered him like a blanket. So the winter passed. When the rivers flooded the wood with the first waters of the thaw, the noise of the torrent woke him. He was dragged past trees rotten with frost, past drowned animals and drifting rafts. By the time he reached the shore it was spring. He suddenly remembered what light was like; a sky of purest blue in which the brilliance of the sun floated in tiny particles. He drank in that light, feeling it flood into his mouth, flow through his arteries, restoring life to every part of his body.

It was a month of splendour. He stayed in a beach hut which resembled a temple and, at night, seemed to cast a shadow over the whole region. He watched the splendid summer evenings, when the sun seemed to tremble convulsively on the horizon, gushing blood that coagulated in a gigantic arc of elemental colours. He exposed his wounds to the light and, one by one, the scabs fell away to reveal new skin. He lived on the sap of plants and the water flowing over the stones. One day a man came to meet him:

'Don't you know me? Perhaps you don't recognize my face because of this habit I'm wearing, or perhaps my voice has grown hoarser over the years. But I'm still prepared to help you. Do you wish to pass through the final doors? God lives on the other side. It's a vast plain in whose dust you can still make out the footprints left by the ancient knights. None of them returned, but once a message came back. It said: "Nothing is as we expected it to be." I racked my brains trying to interpret it. A lot of work and all to no avail. But they're waiting for us on the other side. Every now and then I receive a request. Nothing concrete: an inner voice. A mystic? Yes, in a way, although my contact is not directly with the divinity. It's something coarser than that. Besides, I like women. I enjoy dousing them with sacrificial wine and watching them writhe in ecstasy. When they fall asleep, I undress them. I derive immense pleasure from the sight of inert bodies. Sometimes, I lie on my side until my arm goes numb. Then I can burn it, slash it, flail it with nettles. I know that the pain will come later, that is the desired punishment. Those are the ritual's finest moments – the slow return of the circulation and, with it, unbearable pain.'

He left the man sitting on a rock, talking to himself. The dull green, almost black, of the cedars and cypresses combines with the onset of night. He went through the arched doorway that led into a flowerless, labyrinthine garden full of covered avenues and sombre statues fatuously waving their hands, trying to grasp the shadows of the small, swift clouds that the branches of the trees alternately concealed and revealed, as if the sky were a dark, silent hallway and the soul were hidden beneath a black hood.

5

From the door, he sees the sea. The distance that separates him from it is marked by a stony, muddy path, crossed by a stream so swollen by the recent thaw that it's barely passable. Nevertheless, he plunged into the water, as befitted his role as exile driven from one of reason's shores by the inertia of the gods.

When he reached the other side, he stopped and, in accordance with the time-honoured rite, looked back. His soul lay fallen by some trees, like a thrush caught in a snare. It was even paler than usual. He tried to shout out his name, but the noise of the current drowned his voice. Then, turning towards the sea, he began to run towards the sun that wrapped him in a purple haze. It was like floating in a dimension of pure light, a light that welled up out of him like a flood of turbid water in which he floundered as he struggled to free himself, only succeeding in plunging further in.

He had a sense of abysmal depths. The sea before him became thick as whitewash, full of scraps of seaweed torn into shreds by an invisible churning. He stared at the horizon. It looked like a scene out of the Apocalypse. The whole universe turned upon a few threads of mist dessicated by the winds of eternity, while below them lay the semicircle of horizon like a skull seared by fire and salt.

He fled, taking with him the last shadows of the night and avoiding the pale light that announced the arrival of the dawn.

6

He woke as the train was entering the last tunnel. Its black walls amplified the train's final whistle, wounding ears that had seemed impervious to all aggression. He looked out of the window and the glass reflected back at him the image of his own face. 'Is this the end of the journey then? A face mingling with my own face, looking back at me as if I were a stranger, as if it wanted to drive me from myself?' He tried to wake the man sitting opposite: 'We're nearly there!' But the man was locked fast in some unknown region of sleep, his head swaying to the rhythm of the tracks, now gradually diminishing in intensity.

Suddenly light flooded the compartment. The train was leaving the tunnel and was now almost through to the other side of the mountain. The climate of the south assailed him with all its usual exhibitionist joy, offering him a landscape of small, cultivated fields and neat, well-kept houses, hinting at a comfortable, tidy world with no room for disquiet or ghosts. Then the scene changed: factories, walls concealing fast roads, deserted warehouses. The train enters the station and suddenly everyone is heaving their baggage out into the corridor, crowding around the doors, leaving behind them their night-time fears. He watched them jump down on to the platform, embracing the people waiting for them, who, to judge by the shouts and occasional tears, they hadn't seen for ages. None of this took much time and, within a few minutes, both compartment and platform were empty.

He looked at the window again. Although both the tunnel and the night had been left behind, his image was still there. He was reluctant to tear himself away from it. But at last, he did, setting off in the direction of the city, still unable to justify this definitive abandonment of a part of his own self.

SWEDEN

The New Country

ANA VALDÉS

translated by Joan Tate

She should have been a cartographer, the kind of person who draws maps and borders with the aid of compass and surveyor's instruments. The family laughed when she minutely cut up her meat until all the pieces looked alike. 'What a methodical girl,' cried her grandfather. The sharp knife fondly followed the marbled surface of the meat, which looked like hieroglyphics on red papyrus. The unknown had always attracted her.

The girl collected maps and travel accounts, wandering with Burton through black Africa, sailing with Alvar Nuñez Cabeza de Vacas on ill-fated expeditions, climbing with Amundsen and Scott over snow-covered mountains. There was room for the whole world inside Grandfather's worn old bound books from which she had learnt to read when she was five.

But life required something else of her. In August, when she arrived at the little airport in Växsjö, for the first time she felt that she was in an unknown landscape, that the names on the map resembled nothing she had learnt before. That worried the girl with the dark gaze.

She looked around, but couldn't find the courage to take a single step, almost paralysed with grief. An observant spectator would have been able to see (but only for a fleeting second, her self-control was so great) the way her face had become young and innocent again, freed from the weighty burden of the journey, from the mask that made her look older than her twenty-four years.

The airport was deserted, silent and sleepy, a contented cat sleeping off its dinner. But a few cars and a small welcoming committee were there and she was taken to an even smaller place, Alvesta.

She learnt later that this new country was divided into many different small lands, Ångermanland, Småland, but deep down she had christened it Nomansland, the land that is not.

Again she smelt the indescribable scent that had followed her since childhood; her own native country was also much of a nomansland, squeezed like a wedge between two giants, invisible, borderless like the kingdom of dreams. 'Fool's Paradise' someone had called it.

The characteristic scent of nomanslands was nothing that could be explained in words; it smelt like a stillborn child, a shattered jar, burnt bread.

She thought Lazarus must have had the same smell when he rose from the tomb. Martha and Mary scrubbed after him, burnt incense, opened jars of fragrance, but nothing helped. He brought with him a strange perfume from the tomb, from the threshold between the living and the dead.

She came to her new country on 21 August, only a few days after her birthday. She had scarcely noticed it, not to mention celebrated it. Later she was to find that memories manage to sift out the unpleasant, the uncomfortable, the sorrowful, the mad.

The journey had been nightmarish, a study in humiliation and uncertainty. She was one of thirty who had been granted asylum in Sweden, at least fifteen of them small children. They had neither passports nor money, and were travelling with papers from the United Nations which guaranteed them a new country. It was to be as if being born anew, the enthusiastic official at the Embassy had said.

Frankfurt Airport was frightening and unfriendly. Her

elementary English and her school German were just sufficient to negotiate for an empty waiting room where the mothers could feed their babies and change nappies, where the nervous men could smoke as they had smoked when they had had their first child.

Nearly all of them were descendants of European peasants and workers who had sought happiness in America. They had come in great ships, laden with heavy chests. They had sold their patch of land to siblings and cousins. Yellowing certificates stated where they came from, what their names were, whom they had married. Old grandfather Francesco venerated an army testimony, signed by King Vittorio Emanuele, in which he is praised for his 'courageous contributions in the war'.

But old Grandfather, grown tired of war in distant places, Abyssinia, Eritrea, Istanbul, Montenegro, had sought out calmer territories.

Now their grandchildren were again making the journey. Like a circle closing, a dog chasing its own tail, they were shadows of their forefathers, constantly seeking happiness.

Later she was to realize that happiness is like grains of sand flying in the wind when the shore is emptied of people, that happiness is like a Tivoli after closing time, a lighthouse no longer showing lost ships the way, a faceless carnival mask lifted out of the shadows.

This was one of the least populated places in northern Europe, far away from the Italy of her parents or from the Bavaria of her nuns. The nuns had taught her geography with maps from 1942. During her entire childhood, she and her school friends had thought Europe consisted of one great country, Germany, and a few other small insignificant places.

The nuns taught her that in northern Europe there lived some barbaric tribes who spoke various dialects stemming from German and lived off reindeer and fish. Polar bears roamed the town streets and people travelled on skis along frozen streets and across market squares.

She quickly learnt to recognize certain scents. New scents, quite unlike anything she had smelt before. The trees smelt like dull violins, the water left a vague taste of chlorine and chemicals, people smelt different, rather paler, rather muter. But she was soon able to distinguish and love the new scents, burnt birchwood, thawing snow, fallen leaves in autumn, wet soles of leather boots, the scents of lilac and honeysuckle, the perfume of lily-of-the-valley.

It was strange, but she had never learnt the names of flowers and trees in her own language. To her mother, a tree was a tree, not a specific and unique creature, as complete as a human being.

After a while in the new country, the postman became the most important person in her life. She looked out for his bicycle, counting how many minutes he stopped at other houses, sulking when he was asked in for coffee or delayed by a talkative old person. She and old people were the only ones sitting waiting at home. The old people often talked about the old days, when the post came twice a day, the morning delivery, the afternoon post, the mail order catalogues from which you buy everything from a jersey to an electric drill.

She was ill and alone, homesick, longing back to her dead grandparents, to their house, to the house Grandfather had had built for his family, the house which had been her childhood fortress, protecting her from the world. The house which was always inhabited, open to all, a refuge for abandoned cats of the district, and lost girls, whom Grandmother took under her wing and they became her nursemaids.

Home to the town she had naively believed was the centre of the universe, to the mighty river as wide as a sea. Receiving letters was the only thing that healed her. She was the district doctor's favourite patient, challenging his knowledge and talents, making him go on reading books he hadn't touched since his student days.

Physically she was perfectly healthy, her blood count normal, her reflexes good, her organs and cells showing no sign of mortal change, but all the same, she was wasting away like a fish taken out of water, a piece of ice melting in the hot sun.

Fish species were also something she learnt about here, in her new country. Perch, pike, angler-fish, pike-perch, whitefish, cod, sole, carp, roach, plaice, swordfish, salmon, burbot, char, trout, haddock, turbot.

At first the doctor thought she was the victim of a tropical disease; he saw himself as a new Albert Schweitzer victoriously taking her off to various medical congresses. He would cure her melancholy and be mentioned in books and journals all over the world. His disappointment was great when she pointed at the map of her native country, almost as far from the tropics as his own.

Her mother was well, her father sent his love, her little nephew asked when she was coming back. They had taught him to look up and identify the planes of the various airlines. 'Look, there goes Lufthansa. Can you see the bird?'

The winter had been cold and windy, the white beaches of Rio de la Plata rigid and frozen like blocks of ice; some fishermen said they had seen sharks and a small whale. That wouldn't surprise her – in the days of Claes Gill, back in the twenties, Montevideo had been the last outpost of the whale. As all the indications now pointed to time being out of joint and moving backwards, it was not impossible that the sea around Uruguay would again be allowed to provide shelter to sharks and killer whales, dolphins and seals.

She thought about her birthdays, hot chocolate and cold hands that could not find the curly ends, could not open her presents in any way except with scissors that cut through the difficult knots.

She had never been good at handwork. The nuns tried in vain to teach her embroidery. They showed her lovely ornamented cassocks, purple for Holy Week, red and white for the Resurrection and Baptism, green and black for all the solemn ceremonies of the year.

How had she ended up here, so far away from home? But none the less the new landscape was not alien. The endless expanses also belonged to her country, though there they were green and here they were as white as sheets.

Like the white sheet with which many years later she was to cover her mother's face, the sheet she had lifted in the naive hope of seeing someone else's face and that a cruel joker had been playing a trick on her.

Behind the carnival mask were hidden her mother's fine features, so like her own. Arlecchino, Pulcinella, Pierrot, a masquerade with shadows, a theatre built by a mad king for his mistress. Death had enamelled her mother in soft pastel colours, the brittle bones glowing through the cheeks; she was illuminated from within. Who is holding that lantern?

She thought of herself as Siegfried, that her mother and her grandmother had made her invulnerable and their invocations would for ever protect her from pain and death, from sorrow and loneliness.

But people now found themselves at the end of time, in times the Book of Revelations had already announced.

Gene-manipulated calves and implanted pigs' hearts, castrated pederasts, sectioned schizophrenics, all AIDS sufferers, those who prayed and swore in three thousand languages to hundreds of different gods, to ikons and statuettes representing gods with dog-heads, gods with bull necks, gods with serpent bodies.

'A mighty king shall come. His kingdom shall maketh other kingdoms into shadows, other kings shall kneel before his glory and say: "here is my sword, for you are the King of Kings. Be merciful to us."'

But no one had shown them mercy, their houses were burnt down, their most beloved possessions scattered to the winds – Grandfather's books on insects and chemical formulae, Father's riding whip, Mother's handwritten cookery book – and they themselves had been taken prisoner.

'By the waters of Babylon we sang of our vanished friends, of our disappointments, of our fear.'

Now only letters from home became her link with the outside world. All letters that came were received with solemn ceremonies. First, look at the sender. Then, look at the stamps and investigate which day the letter had been posted. Sometimes bizarre letters came, from authorities or organizations wanting her to do this, that or the other, go for a medical check-up, to group therapy, support-group counselling, an association meeting, a church coffee morning, a neighbourhood gathering, a Co-operative Society meeting, a party congress, a parent-teacher meeting, consultation with the teacher, someone's hen-party, a fortieth birthday party, a wedding.

She had not felt that important before; at home with her grandparents no importance was attached to children. They were at an intermediate station, childhood a kind of waiting room for adult life.

Letters were something unknown to her. She had never previously written letters, received letters, worked, had a house of her own, paid rent, received a salary. Everything was so new to her, so unique. She felt chosen; fate had chosen her among so many others, like being born anew, the official had said, the same official who had described the new country as an idyll, with little red houses and good kind people who would invite her to coffee and homemade buns.

She would sit on the parlour sofa and look at photographs of 'what it was like before', when this country had been emptied of people who went away, when lice and scurvy were common, when backward people were sterilized, when eyes were closed to Red Cross wagons filled with arms, where Povel Ramel was young and time was still a promise, when Ingvar Kamprad cycled round Småland and sold seeds and condoms.

She was like a young knight watching over his spurs, afraid of making a fool of herself, tense and wondering. Was there a life after this? Would all these people like me, consider me worthy of sharing their happiness?

Of course it was a happiness to live in a country where they could all say what they wanted, where no one was imprisoned for his or her opinions, where freedom prevailed, where everyone (at least on paper) had the right to work and a place to live, to free education and a secure old age.

She was born in a melancholy town, where the sky changed colour a hundred times, where voices sounded polite but slightly cool, where smiles were slightly strained, where the air was thin and as sharp as a scalpel. Her home town's music was Satie's sorrowful cracked tunes, an abandoned harbour where skeletons of ships dream of other days and other places, a woman running and losing a shoe, a choir singing in an empty church. Allegro, minor, piano, pianissimo. In Montevideo's symphony there was neither staccato nor fortissimo.

That was what was most difficult, learning the voice of the new town. The tune could at first mislead, making the stranger think this time it was also melancholy and weary. But to the trained ear, it was easy to make out that was only a curtain of mist, that the new country was as savage and forceful as a young centaur not yet decided whether he is human or animal.

The country was as heathen and barbaric as a cave painting. Their gods were the young warriors condemned to endless fighting in the eternal paradise of the battlefield. She felt a thousand years older than her new countrymen; she was born in a churchyard with old trams and ancient cafés where the castaways from the whole world's shipwrecks had gathered to remember, where palace and patrician apartments had been taken over by rats and bats, like a film set left behind after the film crew has gone home, where predatory animals and wild dogs gnawed at nameless bones.

For lack of any other material, the bridge between the two towns was built of stacked shoe-boxes and extended over a desolate landscape, covered with ice and reeking lava. She had to cross the bridge with cautious steps, for one false step would banish her into oblivion, to nothing.

Sometimes she sought in vain to remember what she was like when young, what she was like as a girl, as a child. She had asked older aunts and cousins, but was given only disconnected details, taken out of context.

The picture became blurred, one of those sepia coloured photographs of Grandmother as a sixteen-year-old beauty. So beautiful 'the bells rang for her as she went past', her grandfather used to say.

With an effort, she was able to trace herself as an adolescent, a stubborn dreamy child, always reading. As a hunting hound sniffs eagerly at the place where the prey has stopped to collect itself, she felt like that whenever a small detail from her past appeared. The definition increased, and an old picture swam in the developer.

Her first ball, the red dress, dancing with older brothers of school friends, secret smoking, her younger sister, a growing shadow, a clumsy colt. Every day she asked the mirror who she was; she had no desire to risk forgetting. So many people woke in the morning without knowing who they were, where they came from, in what language they usually said: 'Good morning'.

The mirror always responded with references, a tired sibyl constantly forgetting the ritual words, who would have preferred to have gone on sleeping undisturbed: 'you are the daughter of Helena, grandchild of Ophelia, cousin of Pablo, of Pedro, of José. You were born under Leo one early morning in August. It was cold and your mother was afraid; you looked at her with dark accusing eyes. She maintains you did not wish to be born. The sun was in Leo then, as was the moon, Venus and Mars. So you have a great deal of fire. You will die young, of spontaneous combustion.'

Grandmother was the only one who could handle her fire. She was cool and as sharp as a diamond pin and scratched unforgettable traces in the girl's soul, invisible to others, written in a secret code only the two of them knew. Her flame grew tame and warm whenever Grandmother was near, her presence enough to set limits to the mad dance of the fire.

But in the new country, the mirror had been almost mute and the memories of Grandmother paler. So few people knew her by name, so few knew who her parents were, in which house they lived, whether they were old or young, whether they loved her.

Her name was also a worry. At all costs, she wished to avoid being known by her real name, the holy name her mother had given her when expecting her.

She herself had almost forgotten it until she heard her mother whispering it again, before she went away into the kingdom of mist, to the place where time and place are united, to the eye of the storm, the only place in the world that could be called home.

But at the same time, she longed for someone to whom she could tell that secret name. The chosen one would know everything about her, everything about her tangled inner geography, where there were rivers that often overflowed, high inaccessible mountains, dark fragrant valleys, narrow paths, abandoned towns, plundered churches, soured lakes, polluted shores, remains everywhere. Dusty ruins of magnificent dreams, ash from burnt-out bodies, the sweet-sour scent of decayed corpses, pale and half-eaten human bodies.

'Thou shalt not consume that flesh. Thy lips shall not taste this blood.' But man is the wolf of man, and now no one was safe.

Vampires and arms dealers, assassins and cannibals, mercenaries and werewolves, false prophets and corrupt politicians, bribable policemen and uniformed butchers. The horsemen of war were already on their way to the meeting decided on since the beginning of time, the horsemen of disease and hunger spurring on their swift steeds, the horsemen of death already there.

Her new freedom intoxicated her, no family to see to, no voices telling her what was right, what was wrong. Her future was no longer determined, and she could be whatever she liked. No lawyer's office waiting for her degree, no inherited posts, no convent school to teach in.

She was like a tightrope walker walking a taut rope high above the ground with no safety net, somewhat shaken by all that was new, but for the first time ever one with herself, concentrated, sharp as a laser beam making holes in the hard steel.

Then she suddenly discovered the language. She was not aware of it before, like a fish swimming but not knowing anything about water; she had been that deaf to the language.

But now the language was something both outside and inside her, a colourful mixture of ritual forms and inherited formulations, a liturgy of ceremonies and actions shaped and sketched when the world was young, when darkness reigned.

'In the principle was the word. And the word created the world.' Let there be light, and the universe was drowned in an explosion of white and yellow, red and green. Let there be earth, and the soil smelt strongly of manure and decaying frogs. Let there be sea and rivers and all inconsiderable streams and lakes flowed like liquid silver. Let there be life and all was filled with cooing, squeaking and lowing. Unicellular animals, four-footed giants, fish and trees, birds and juniper bushes, squirrels and lemon balm.

In the new language, she recreated the world, and not a single one of the words she knew from the old world were put to use.

The old magic formulae seemed to have lost their magical force, no longer meaning anything. She said 'caballo' and no horse appeared. She mumbled 'te quiero' and her beloved did not turn in the wide bed she had bought secondhand. Only scars from Grandmother's sharp character continued to live within her, independent of the new order, as immovable as the gates of Troy before the fateful horse had been allowed in.

Her language had become a Janus face, one half pointing towards the past, the other pointing to the future, which was not yet.

But this new idiom did not become the language of her heart until she met the chosen one. He had infected her with a desire for language she had never felt before. She craved it with the same passion as she craved his soul. She wanted to drown in the new language with the same intoxicated joy she allowed herself drown in the skin of her loved one, in the scents of her beloved. Lemon and myrrh, sea-salt and freshly ground coffee, burnt sugar and vanilla, warm new-laid eggs.

The language lit in her a flame that spread sparks of warmth and light wherever she found herself. She was like a bonfire on Walpurgis Night, a homage to life and what is secret, to the magic formulae that the new tongue had given her, to the new world which allowed itself to be renamed by her groping words.

The new world took no notice of grammatical norms or rules of spelling. She was a sorcerer's apprentice, who one day would be initiated into and in agreement with all the secrets of the language, its most hidden nuances, in the holy of holies, the chamber where the language cared for what was not yet born, what had not been mentioned before, what was patiently waiting to be discovered.

With the same childish curiosity that had marked the

descriptions by chroniclers of the new world they had discovered, she wrote letters home with stories of her new life.

She surprised her mother when she told her about her sophisticated cooking. Indian dishes, sushi, crème caramel, breadcrumbed cheese, Greek sheep's cheese salad, Turkish cakes, Jansson's Temptation. Iron pans and garlic presses, raw preserving and microwave ovens, so very far from Grandmother's copper pans, from the aunts' home baked tea cakes and thick jams.

Her new life had few points of contact with the old life. The house in the fashionable district of her home town had become an apartment in an anonymous suburb, old leather-bound books cheap paperbacks, the traditional oak and ebony furniture transformed into untreated pine, chipboard, the seasons reversed.

The first snow filled her with wonder, the landscape shrouded in white, lakes frozen, the air itself as sharp as a sword blade.

The town slumbered, like Sleeping Beauty, waiting for spring. Under the snow lived myriads of small creatures, centipedes, worms, beetles, ants. Their almost invisible tracks in the snow helped her find her way home one evening when she had gone astray. It was easy to go astray in this town.

She lived in a suburb built in the sixties, a suburb of several high rise blocks and a few shops. When the shops closed and people hurried home, the streets were deserted and inhospitable. No café to sit in to write poems, no cinema, no food shops open at night.

Sometimes a neighbour's father might come on a visit and say: 'To think that I hunted deer here only thirty years ago. All these buildings, all these cars. There was nothing here but forest and game!'

The neighbour used to invite her back home and there she could taste the culinary delicacies of the country which she usually bought ready-cooked. He worked nights at the post office and studied economics in the daytime. Hash, black pudding, dried fish, potato dumplings, beestings pudding, black soup from goose giblets, veal brawn.

One of her favourite places in the new town was the library. There she could read newspapers and books written in all the languages of the world. She borrowed books and took them home. Many of them she had read before, but she wanted to see what they were like in the new language. Did Camus sound the same in Swedish, was Virginia Woolf as gripping in the new language?

Once she had joined them in the longest queue, patiently waiting to be allowed to read a paper. They were mostly older men, all a trifle sorrowful, as if in exile. When her turn came, she found that the newspaper was the *Västerbotten Courier*, a local paper in Norrland.

The girl asked the librarian why so many people wanted to read just that newspaper, full of local news. The librarian patiently explained that most of those men were born up in Norrland and they had had to move to the city to find work. They had never felt at home in the suburbs of the city and longed for the forest, the wide expanses and the great lakes.

They read the newspaper for news from home, to see who had married, who had had children, who had died. One day they would go back.

She recognized the feeling. She had felt like that for the first years. Then the memory of home faded, ties and feelings weakened. When she had finally been given permission to return, she found to her horror that there was nothing to go back to, the home town she remembered had gone, wiped off the earth. The cafés had become video game arcades, theatres had become assembly halls, cinemas discotheques, and the prison where she had spent four long years had been turned into a vocational school.

Friends had grown up and become strangers, school

friends had become diplomats' wives and politicians, someone had committed suicide.

Her first boyfriend, now a young grandfather divorced for the third time, was drowning his sorrows in drink. He also mourned the vanished town where he had written his best poems, where they had played chess with old Hungarian masters, castaways from all the wars of the world.

She felt all towns were alike, scenery for human lives, for all the plays of everyday drama. Tragedies and comedies followed one another in a perpetual performance changing place and time.

She was an exile from a time and not from a place. Nomad against her will, she searched like Proust for a vanished time, a time when everything had seemed clearer and cleaner, full of trust. A time in which everyone had called one another brothers and sisters, in which the Messiah had a beard and a beret and had taken his asthma medicine into the jungle, in which paradise lay round the corner and where all antagonisms were allowed to exist.

But she would take the consequences. Although the new time offered no truths, although the new time was a lonely place to be in, although the tune of the new time sounded alien to her ears, she did not want to flee.

Life wanted her to cope, as witness from another time, from another place in the world. Like an animal which through a genetic mutation gives birth to another animal in a later generation, better prepared for the new climate, better equipped for the new conditions of the world, more intelligent, sharper, humbler, that was how she would be. The girl felt she was a hybrid, a mixture of fish and lizard, belonging both on land and in water, an arrow flying through the air but not yet reached the target.

She was still a sketch, a will, an unspoken dream. For the first time she felt she was not afraid that the one who was dreaming her would wake. In the new town, among all these new people, she knew the dream was her own, and she need not be anxious.

The dream of herself was more real than all scenery.

IRELAND

Florida Coast

BRIAN LEYDEN

All she had eaten since she got up was a crust of brown bread with a scrape of orange marmalade and a mug of hot tea. Hot tea was an addiction – coloured with milk and sweetened with a half-spoon of sugar. It cured her headaches in the morning and helped her to relax when she was alone in the house at night.

Her guts were rattling but the morning jobs were done. She was pulling off her waterproofs and wellington boots when the telephone in the kitchen chimed.

'Hello, Ellen.'

'Maureen, how are you? It's great to hear your voice. You must have known I was thinking about you.'

'Is everything all right?'

'When were things ever all right in Ireland? How is everybody in America?'

'We're all fine. Joseph and his wife were up for a few days from Chicago, and I had our old neighbour George Oliver and his wife Molly over.'

'I thought that man was dead and buried.'

'He was meeting friends from home at the airport. I had them stay with me for a couple of days. It was just like old times.'

'Visitors can be a big strain, Maureen, especially if you're the one has to do all the entertaining. You must be worn out.'

'Are you kidding? I looked forward to getting in from work and finding someone in the house. The place feels so empty since Susan's wedding. Especially at night. And there are all kinds of bums hanging round the neighbourhood.'

'I've got a few hops here on my own. Last night I thought I heard someone walking around under my window.'

'Did you call for the cops?'

'It was only a badger,' Ellen said. 'He put the heart crossways in me.' It would have upset Maureen if she confessed how severely her courage had been tested.

'Why don't you come over, Ellen?'

'You know I can't get away.'

'What's holding you? You're a widow woman. The boys have married and moved out. And you've never been to my house in America.'

'It's a rest I need, Maureen, not travel. I'm cold and I'm tired the whole time, and I'd want to put horse-nails in my soup I'm that short of iron.'

'You've got to look after your health. I'll buy vitamins and we'll drive down to Florida. You can pick your own oranges in the back garden.'

'God, I don't know, Maureen.'

'I'll send you the dollars. Or I can book the trip from here and send the ticket.'

'It's not the expense.'

'What's holding you then?'

'The cattle.'

'Sell the lousy cattle!'

'Someone has to look after the farm, Maureen. It's not just the cattle. If I don't clear the land now the place will be taken over with weeds. I cut a square every dry hour I get. It's thankless work, I know. Like dusting, it doesn't stay done long. But it has to be done all the same.'

'Ask some of the boys to come back and look after the place for a while.'

'They have their own lives, Maureen.'

'What about the neighbours?'

How could she explain to her sister that animals were like small children: most people would volunteer to look after them for a day or two, but not for a week or a fortnight.

'It's very good of you to ask, Maureen, but you'll have to let me think about it. Why don't I write? This call must be costing you a fortune.'

'I'm not worried about the price of a phonecall.'

'I don't see how I can get away. The barn needs a new door. And I had the expense of putting in the phone this year.'

'I told you not to worry about the money. I'll pay for the trip.'

'I'll have to wait until the spring calves are stronger.'

'I'll send you the dollars anyway.'

'I'll only send them back.'

'What's a few lousy bucks? I'll call again in a week.'

'Ah Jasus, now what am I going to do?' Ellen asked herself as she put down the phone.

In the back of the cupboard in the kitchen there was an album bulging with purple-tinted, Eastman Kodak Company colour photographs. Family pictures going back over the years. Ellen opened the album to look for a photograph of George Oliver and Molly.

The pictures were stuck down at random but several had scribbled dates and titles: August 23rd 1957. Rockaway. Jones beach. Labour Day 1964. A visit to the World Fair. Independence Day and Thanksgiving dinners.

Maureen and her friends were pictured at big American weddings drinking from crystal goblets, seated before oval platters of food on spreads of white linen and silverware shining. In the photographs Maureen was the same age and had the same clear features as her married daughter, Susan, today.

Ellen's second sister, Delia, was pictured in tartan shorts showing a sun-tanned leg on a scorched lawn before a clapboard house with a sun-porch and wooden steps leading up to the screen door. Their husbands were more proudly posed for the instamatic camera, each with a foot up on the fender of an enormous, chrome-finished American car. Both men wore big, bright, double-breasted suits, sharply creased.

A friend of Maureen's stood in the centre of a large apartment furnished with a deep-pile carpet and matching sofa and armchairs. There were books and pictures of the Catskill mountains on the walls in place of the farm almanacs, holy effigies and Mission calendars found at home. The girl stood with one hand on her hip and one hand lightly rested on the new television set. She wore a short white fur-trimmed coat, white elbow-length gloves and pearls.

'Just get-a-load-a-me,' the picture said.

President John F. Kennedy's people; prosperous, white Irish-Americans settled in Great Neck and Long Island, Chicago and Boston, Connecticut and Washington. Doing well. Proud of their rising fortunes.

These tantalizing shots of the good life waiting on the other side of the Atlantic came regularly in the heavy parcels from America packed with clothes: consolation outfits for the brothers and sisters who were stuck at home on the farm. The frocks and skirts were dazzling and smelled of camphor mothballs and ozone after their slow sea crossing by second-class post. The dresses looked fabulous in the photographs taken on the sidewalks of America under the native maples: between the bare hawthorn hedges and the muddy lanes of Ireland the sequins, the lamé, the taffeta, the gold and silver embroidery and flyaway fabrics looked like last year's Christmas tree thrown out in the yard.

The photographs from home were different. Down-at-heel and undated, 3 × 2 inch, black-and-white prints taken under wet skies. There was one of Ellen and her mother posed in sturdy foursquare buttoned coats. She looked chubby with no make-up. And the only sign of prosperity in the whole collection was a tall old-fashioned car, registration IT 809. It might have been one of Henry Ford's original Model Ts it looked so old, with a rusty hole eaten in the right-hand mudguard and the owners' faces lost behind the horizontal bar in the middle of the folding windshield.

There was no shortage of handsome and shy boys nearing manhood, squinting down the lens of the Box Brownie. Photographed in their shabby best suits, their shirts collarless, their jackets open, standing at the gables of rough stone cottages with tiny windows. And each had the look of youths who were next for America.

'Come over, come and join us. Look how we dress. Look how well we eat. Look how we fit the part,' said the people in the colour pictures.

They wanted their brothers and sisters over, and they baited the hook with these snapshots of prosperity, sent back the Cunard line menus and other souvenirs from their sea passage and used the bright lure of American glamour as they stood waiting on that far shore to haul the next arrivals in.

Strange then how they could never truly break that connection with the green world of the past. That deep bond of guilt or fondness. A lasting strain of homesickness remained for small cottages and half-doors. A sentimental longing for that half-acre patch of oats standing in stooks beside the spud ground that bordered the dog-daisy and sweet-grass meadows. The golden barley straw thatched roofs, the whitewashed walls and the outhouses painted with farmers' green- and red-lead paint that formed a picture in their souls more lasting than all those tinted Eastman Kodak snapshots.

When they hit pay-dirt in America they came looking for that vision again using the strong dollar. They were extravagant and generous with the payrolls earned from working double shifts and taking second jobs at night. The money went on package travel, hired cars and that truly unique American largesse.

These visits were lovingly recorded in the album. There was Ellen's young brother, Joseph, looking like Elvis Presley with his coal-black sideburns and his hair combed back. His American wife wearing the latest beehive hair-do. A brand new Pilot valve radio on the high shelf in the kitchen.

Ellen's two young boys were pictured there, too, teasing or caught fighting a running battle with their so much more sturdy and better dressed cousins from America. They had worn paths to the shed where the crates of Coca Cola, bought by their uncle to last the fortnight's holiday, were stored in the cool dark outhouse called the dairy.

'Jeez, you guys can drink soda,' their uncle had marvelled as they belched to relieve their gas-swollen bellies, standing beside the stack of crates emptied by the second day.

There were more crates of beer and cartons of Kent duty-free cigarettes in foil packets for the neighbours and the far out relations who came to sit with drinks in their hands in the kitchen. And the stay-at-home girls with plain faces, bad teeth and straight hair were invited to squeeze their Hohner accordions as the couples stepped out a dance on the lino, while the old men toasted each other with shot-glasses of whiskey in the back-kitchen.

A special journey had to be made to buy a fridge to replace the square, metal meat-safe with the tiny ventilation holes in the sides. The new white fridge had a moulded rack in the door to hold eggs, a plastic tray to make ice-cubes in the freezing compartment at the top, and shelves to hold the leg of lamb bought for the farewell dinner.

Then the Americans got up at five in the morning for the drive to Shannon airport and the return flight to New York via Boston. Fighting the battle of the bulge with a squadron of plaid suitcases packed with Waterford Crystal, Irish bacon and sausages, processed cheese, plain milk chocolate and white wool Aran sweaters.

Ellen might have gone with them after any one of these visits, but she stayed at home.

'The place will be there when you get back,' they said, but someone had to take care of the farm after Maureen and Delia and Joseph married and settled in America.

She was ready to put the photographs away when she found the picture of Molly and George Oliver shaking hands with Mayor Daly shortly after they moved to Chicago. Beside it was an earlier picture, of George Oliver and Ellen's brother Joseph holding up two hayforks on a high summer's day half a lifetime ago. It was a minute or more before the memory of that day returned and when it did it struck Ellen with such force it made up her mind.

George Oliver and Joseph had been sharpening the prongs of their pitchforks, with the whole hard hay-saving day before them, when the American visitors arrived: two women in a big white rented car the full width of the lane.

The older woman was a widow called Molly McFee. She was travelling with her daughter, Judy.

'Hi there,' said the Americans.

'Hello, how are ya?' said Joseph and George Oliver.

The Americans were looking for their ancestors.

'The McFee family,' said George Oliver and he twisted the cap back on his head. There had been no family by the name of McFee in the parish for at least five generations. But George Oliver was a kind soul and he felt a small deception would be better than disappointment.

'All that's left of the McFee's old home is right there,' he said, pointing to the cowbarn.

Thatched, whitewashed and aged, it was the humble birthplace Molly had always imagined. 'Thank you so much,' she said after the pictures were taken, and she began to pull off notes from a wad of dollars.

'Put that money back in your pocketbook,' George Oliver said firmly.

'But you must have something,' Molly insisted.

She had planned a trip to the seaside to round off the day. George Oliver and the young man had been so kind and so helpful. Why not come along? There was no question whose dollars would be used to pick up the bills.

'I'd like to oblige,' George Oliver said. 'But I have a big field to hay down.'

Joseph's eyes had never left young Judy. He was wearing a plaid shirt and baggy working trousers but he was a fine looking youth and well built for his age. Judy was California brown with twists of sun-gold hair. She was exotic yet friendly, foreign and still remarkably innocent. And she seemed to like him. But George Oliver's field of hay had been cut four days ago, and wet lumps scattered with pitchforks and then turned twice with wooden hay-rakes. It would be cracking dry.

'It is really ready for harvesting?' Molly asked George Oliver as she patted her hair and inspected her make-up in the mirror of her vanity case.

'We'll take another look at it,' George Oliver yielded a little.

George Oliver climbed into the back beside Molly. Judy sat up front and Joseph was given the wheel. He bounced the car over the hard cowtracks and steered through the gap into the hayfield.

George Oliver could be a fussy man fixing the last scollop in the thatch or pointing off a reek of turf against the rain. And he was particular about the quality of the hay he saved and fed to his cattle each winter. With the car door unlatched he went to the middle of the field. The sun throbbed in a clear blue heaven. A warm breeze stirred the burnished wisps. He picked up a handful of hay so dry it broke into chaff in his fist.

George Oliver lifted his eyes from the work. A skylark

hovered over the field. The back door of the car stood open. He thought of that billfold of dollars and the holiday smell of sea air. He looked across at Joseph sitting at the wheel beside Judy, and Molly in the back in her high heels and low-cut blouse, and he released his grip.

'It needs another day,' he said as he sat into the back of the big white car headed for the coast.

It was a long drive though the humid Southern states and the sun was so hot the pavement would burn the soles of your bare feet. There were mangoes and orange trees in the gardens and freshly squeezed orange juice by the gallon. Ellen had adjusted well to these hot latitudes and had even begun to put on weight. At home the spring calves had matured to make sturdy young cattle and the boys were taking it in turns to look after the farm.

They were skirting Tallahassee when Ellen ordered tea at a roadside diner. The waitress brought iced tea in a tall glass with a drinking straw and a coloured umbrella. Ellen bent close to her sister as the girl retreated.

'I'll have to bring her into the kitchen and show her how to boil a kettle,' she confided.

At the next stop she had her own supply and ordered boiling water for her tea-bags. A flavour of home in the subtropical heat.

SPAIN

Everything Bad Comes Back

JAVIER MARÍAS

translated by Margaret Jull Costa

Today I received a letter that reminded me of a friend. It was written by a woman unknown both to myself and to that friend.

I met him fifteen or sixteen years ago and – for no other reason than that he died – stopped seeing him two years ago, not that we ever saw each other with any frequency, given that he lived in Paris and I in Madrid. Although he visited my city only rarely, I used to visit his quite often. However, we first met in neither of those two cities, but in Barcelona, and before that meeting, I had previously read a book of his sent to me by a Madrid publishing house I used to work for as a reader (work, as is usually the case, that was poorly remunerated). There was little likelihood of this novel, or whatever it was, ever being published and I can remember almost nothing about it, except that it revealed a certain inventiveness with words, a strong rhythmic sense and a broad culture (for example, the author knew the word 'wrack') but apart from that it was more or less unintelligible, at least to me. Were I a critic, I would have described him as out-Joycing Joyce, though he was less puerile, or perhaps senile, than the later Joyce, to which his own work bore only a remote resemblance. Nevertheless, I recommended the book for publication and expressed my qualified regard for it in my report. His agent subsequently phoned me (for this writer, whose true vocation seemed to be to remain forever unpublished, none the less had an agent) to arrange a meeting to coincide with a trip his client would be making to Barcelona, where his family lived and where, fifteen or sixteen years ago, I too was living.

His name was Xavier Comella and I never did ascertain whether the business to which he sometimes referred vaguely as 'the family business' was in fact the chain of clothes shops of the same name in Barcelona (selling mainly sweaters). Given the iconoclastic nature of his writing, I was expecting some wild, bearded individual, some kind of visionary with a penchant for pendants and vaguely Polynesian clothes, but he wasn't like that at all. The man who emerged from the exit of the metro at Tibidabo, where we'd arranged to meet, was only slightly older than myself – I was about twenty-eight or twenty-nine at the time – and much better dressed (I'm a very neat person myself, but he was wearing a tie – with a small knot – and cufflinks, unusual in men of our age and particularly so then); and he had an extraordinarily old-fashioned face, a face – like his writing – straight out of the interwar period. He wore his slightly wavy, blondish hair combed back, like a fighter pilot or a French actor in a black-and-white movie – Gérard Philipe or the young Jean Marais – and his sherry-brown eyes had a small dark fleck in the white of the left one, which gave his gaze a wounded look. He had good, robust teeth and a well-defined jaw so firm it gave the impression of being permanently clenched. His very prominent cranium, the bones of which were clearly visible beneath the smooth brow, always seemed on the point of exploding, not because of its unusual size, but because the taut skin over the frontal bone seemed incapable of containing it, or perhaps that was just the effect of the two vertical veins at his temples that seemed somehow too protuberant, too blue. He was good-looking, genial and, moreover, extraordinarily polite, especially for a man of his age and given the rather boorish times we lived in. He was one of those men you know you will never be able to confide in, but one in whom you can confidently trust. He had a studiedly foreign, or rather, extraterritorial look about him that only emphasized his estrangement from the times he'd been born into, a look acquired no doubt during the seven or eight years he'd spent out of Spain. He spoke Spanish with the attractive pronunciation of Catalans who have never actually spoken much Catalan (with soft c's and z's, soft g's and j's) and with the slight hint of a stammer at the beginning of sentences, occasionally stumbling over the first three or four words, as if he had to perform some minor mental act of translation. He could speak and read several languages, including Latin, in fact he mentioned that he'd been reading Ovid's *Tristia* on the plane from Paris, and he said this without a trace of pedantry but rather with the satisfaction of one who has mastered some difficult task. He possessed a certain degree of worldly wisdom which he enjoyed showing off; during the long conversation we had in the bar of a nearby hotel, we talked almost exclusively about literature and painting and music, that is, about highly forgettable things, but he did tell me something of his life, about which he always spoke – on that occasion and during all the years we knew each other – with a contradictory blend of discretion and shamelessness. By that I mean that he was prepared to reveal everything or nearly everything, even about very intimate matters, but he always did so with a kind of grave naturalness – or was it perhaps tact? – which, in a way, diminished their importance, like someone who considers that all the strange, sad, terrible, agonizing things that happen to him are perfectly normal, a fate shared by everyone and so, presumably, by the person listening, who will not, therefore, be surprised by what he hears. Not that Xavier eschewed the confessional gesture, but he resorted to it, perhaps, more because he saw it as part of the gestural repertoire of the tormented than because he had any real awareness of what is, at least in principle, untellable. On that first occasion, he told me the following: he'd studied medicine but never practised as a doctor, instead living a life dedicated entirely to literature, funded by a generous inheritance or by some kind of private income, possibly – I can't quite remember now – from a grandfather who owned a textile factory. Whatever the origin of the money, he enjoyed the use of it and had lived off it for the seven or eight years he'd spent in Paris – a move indeed made possible by that money – fleeing from what he considered to be the mediocrity and flaccidity of intellectual life in Barcelona, which, given how young he was when he left, he really only knew about through the press. (Although he grew up in Barcelona, he was born in Madrid, where his mother came from.)

In Paris he'd married a woman called Eliane (he always referred to her by name, I never once heard him call her 'my wife'), who, according to him, had the most exquisite colour sense he'd ever come across in a fellow human being (I didn't ask at the time, but I presumed that she must be a painter). He had a wide-ranging and ambitious literary plan of which, he remarked precisely, he had so far completed about 20 per cent, although none of it had as yet been published. Apart from the people closest to him, I was the first person to have shown any interest in his writings, which comprised novels, essays, sonnets and plays, even a play for puppets. He obviously thought that my opinion held considerable sway at the head office of the publishing house, not realizing that mine was only one voice among many and, given my youth, far from being one of the most influential. He gave me the impression that he was reasonably happy, whatever that means: he seemed to be very much in love with his wife; he was living in Paris whereas, in Spain, we were only just getting over Franco, or so people said; he didn't have to work, his only obligations being those he imposed upon himself; and he doubtless enjoyed a pleasant and interesting social life. And yet, even at our first meeting, I sensed something turbulent and uneasy about him, as if he were surrounded by a cloud of suffering, like a cloud of dust, that gradually gathered about him only to be shaken off afterwards and left behind. When he described to me the amount of work he put into his writing, the endless hours spent labouring over every one of those pages I had read, I thought it was nothing more than that, a concept of writing as old-fashioned as he was himself, a concept that was almost 'pathetic', in the original sense of that word: a summoning up of the pain required to make words, regardless of meaning, communicate intense emotion, the way, he said, that music or pure colour do, or the way mathematics is supposed to. I asked him if he'd also spent hours on one of his rather easier pages to remember, which consisted of the word 'riding' repeated five times on each line, thus:

riding riding riding riding riding

He looked at me with ingenuous eyes, surprised, and then, after a few seconds, he burst out laughing: 'No,' he said, 'of course I didn't.' Then he added, with unexpected simplicity: 'You do say some funny things,' and started laughing again.

He was always rather slow on the uptake when it came to the jokes or, rather, the gentle leg-pulls I allowed myself, especially later on, simply as a way of lessening the intensity of whatever he was telling me. It was as if he didn't immediately understand the ironic register, as if that too required translation, but then, after a few seconds of bewilderment or assimilation, he would laugh out loud – his laughter was almost femininely openhearted – as if amazed that anyone were capable of making a joke in the middle of a serious, not to say solemn or even dramatic, conversation, and he really appreciated it, both the joke and the capability. This is often the case with people who believe they haven't an ounce of frivolity in them; he did, he simply didn't know it. When I saw his reaction, I ventured another funny remark (I should perhaps explain that this is my principal way of demonstrating my liking and affection for someone), and later I said to him: 'The only thing that's lacking for your life to be idyllic, the sort of life led by characters in a Scott Fitzgerald story before everything turns sour, is for one of your books to be published.' His face darkened slightly at this and I thought that perhaps this was caused by my mention of Fitzgerald, an author who was of even less interest to him than he was to me. He answered me gravely: 'It's more a question of excess than lack.' He paused theatrically, as if debating whether or not to tell me what he was clearly burning to say. I kept silent. So did he (he could withstand silence better than anyone I knew); I broke first. I said: 'What do you mean?' He waited a little longer before replying and then announced: 'I suffer from melancholia.' 'Well, I never,' I said, unable to suppress a smile, 'people who suffer from that are usually people who feel they're over-privileged. But it's such a very ancient illness, it can't be that serious, nothing classical ever is, wouldn't you agree?'

There was rarely any ambiguity in what he said and he hastened to clear up what he judged to have been a misunderstanding. 'I suffer, more or less continually, from depressive melancholia,' he said. 'I'm on medication all the time. That keeps it under control, but if I stopped taking the medication, I would almost certainly kill myself. I already tried to do so once, before I came to live in Paris. It wasn't that any particular misfortune had befallen me, I was just in such terrible mental pain that I couldn't bear to go on living. That could happen to me again at any moment and would happen were I to stop taking the medication. At least that's what they tell me and I imagine they're probably right, after all I'm a doctor too.' He wasn't being melodramatic, he spoke about it quite dispassionately, in the same tone in which he'd told me about everything else. 'What happened?' I asked. 'I was staying at my father's country house in Gerona, near Cassá de la Selva. I aimed a rifle at my chest, holding the rifle butt between my knees. My hands started shaking, I lost my grip, and the bullet embedded itself in a wall instead. I was too young,' he added, by way of an excuse, and gave me an amiable smile. He was a very considerate man and insisted on paying the bill.

We began writing to each other and met whenever I visited Paris. I went there, in order to get over some upset or other, only a few months after our first meeting. I used to stay with an Italian friend, a woman whom I've always found amusing and who has, therefore, always been a source of consolation to me. At the time, the company of Xavier Comella simply interested and entertained me, later it became something that demanded repetition, as happens with those people one comes to count on, even in their absence.

At the time, Xavier was living in his father-in-law's house with his wife Eliane, who was French by birth but Chinese in appearance. She was almost depressingly delicate in the way oriental women are who pride themselves on their refinement, and she was certainly refined. Her fantastic colour sense, so highly praised by her husband, was not deployed on any canvas, but in interior design, although it seemed to me that, up until then, she'd worked mainly on the houses of friends and acquaintances rather than for actual clients, as well as on the design of the restaurant owned by her father, Xavier's father-in-law, a restaurant I never visited but which, according to Xavier, was 'the finest Chinese restaurant in France', not that that's saying very much. When he was with his wife, the natural attentiveness of this man who was in the process of becoming my friend became so exaggerated that, at times, it proved positively irritating: he would ask me not to smoke because cigarette smoke made her feel sick; in cafés we always had to sit out on the covered terraces both to avoid the cigarette smoke and because the air circulated more freely there; we also had to sit so that her back was to the pavement, because the sight of the traffic made her dizzy; we could never go anywhere, not even to a cinema that was even half full, because Eliane was afraid of crowds, nor of course could we ever go to a cellar bar or a night club because that gave her claustrophobia; we also had to avoid any large open spaces, such as the Place Vendôme, because she suffered equally badly from agoraphobia; she couldn't walk or remain standing for any longer than it takes for the lights to change and, if there was a queue at the theatre or a museum, even if it was only a matter of minutes, Xavier would have to accompany Eliane to the nearest café and deposit her there – having first checked that there was no other threat to her safety (this took some time since the threats were so various) – in order that she could wait, seated and safe. What with one thing and another, by the time he got back to me in the queue to keep me company in my slow advance, I'd already got the tickets and we had to go back and find her. By then, of course, she would have ordered some tea and we would have to wait while she drank it. On more than one occasion the show began without us or we were obliged to go round the museum at lightning speed. Going out with the two of them together was rather trying, not only because of all these obligations and inconveniences, but also because adoration is never a pretty sight, still less so when the person doing the adoring is a person for whom one feels a certain regard. It inspires a sense of shame, of embarrassment and, in the case of Xavier Comella, it was like being present at a display – albeit partial – of the most deeply felt corner of his private life, something we can tolerate only in ourselves – just as we can only bear the sight of our own blood, our own nail clippings. And it was perhaps all the more embarrassing because, when you met Eliane, you could understand, or at least imagine, why he felt that way. It wasn't that she was an extraordinary beauty, nor was she exactly talkative (of course, she never asked for or complained about anything because that would have been out of keeping with her refined nature, neither was it necessary: Xavier was a solicitous and punctilious interpreter of her every need). My memory of her is of an utterly vague figure, but her principal charm – which was considerable – probably lay in the fact that, even when she was there before you, she felt like a memory, a blurred and tenuous memory and, as such, harmonious and peaceful, soothing and faintly nostalgic, impossible to grasp. Holding her in your arms must have been like embracing something one has lost, as sometimes happens in dreams. Xavier told me once that he'd been in love with her since he was fourteen years old, I didn't dare ask how or where they'd met at such a tender age, but then I don't ask many questions. A single image of the two of them together predominates over all the others. One morning, we visited an open-air market selling flowers and plants; it began to rain really rather hard, but because the excursion had been specially arranged so that Eliane could buy, among other things, the first peonies of the year, no one even considered looking for shelter, not that there was any, instead Xavier opened his umbrella and took enormous pains to ensure that not a single drop of rain fell on her as she continued on her meticulous and unalterable course, with Xavier following always a couple of paces behind, holding his waterproof vault above her and getting soaked in the process, like a devoted servant inured to such things. I brought up the rear, umbrella-less but not daring to abandon the cortège, like a servant of a lower rank, less committed and quite unrewarded.

When she was not with us, he was more forthcoming, much more than he was in his letters too, which were affectionate but restrained, indeed at times they were so intensely laconic that – like the taut skin and the swollen veins on his forehead – they seemed to presage some explosion, an explosion that would take place outside the envelope, in real life. It was during such a meeting, when Eliane was not with us, that he first spoke to me of the violent rages to which he was subject and which I always found so hard to imagine given that, over the thirteen or fourteen years I knew him, I was never a witness to one, although it's true that we saw each other only infrequently and that his life seems to me now like a defective copy of a book, full of blank pages, or like a city that one has driven through many times before but always at night. Once he told me about a recent visit to Barcelona and how he'd borne in silence for as long as he could his father's absurd words of advice – his father had separated from Xavier's mother and had remarried – and how, then, in a sudden fit of rage, he'd started wrecking the house, hurling furniture against walls, tearing down chandeliers, ripping up paintings, demolishing shelves and, of course, kicking in the television set. No one stopped him; he simply calmed down of his own accord after a few cataclysmic minutes. He took no pleasure in telling me this, but neither did he show any regret or sorrow. I met his father in Paris together with his new Dutch wife, who wore a diamond stud in her nose (a woman ahead of her time). His father's name was Ernest and the only thing he had in common with Xavier was the prominent forehead: he was much taller and had black hair with not a trace of grey in it, possibly dyed, he was a vain man, indulgent and easy-going, but slightly disdainful of his own son, whom he evidently didn't take at all seriously, although that may not have meant much, since he obviously didn't take anything very seriously. He was like an eternal spoiled child, still keen on riding competitions, skeet shooting and – at the time – leafing through treatises on Hindu philosophy; he was one of those people, increasingly rare nowadays, who seemed to spend their entire lives lounging around in silk dressing gowns. Xavier didn't take his father very seriously either, but he couldn't treat him with the same disdain, partly because his father irritated him so much, but also because he just hadn't inherited that particular characteristic.

It was on another occasion when Eliane was absent, about two or three years after our first meeting, that Xavier told me about the death of their newborn child, possibly, I can't quite remember, strangled by its own umbilical cord, but no, it wasn't that, because I recall now one of his extremely rare remarks on the subject (he hadn't even told me they'd been expecting a baby): 'It's much worse for Eliane than it is for me,' he said. 'I don't know how she's going to react. The worst thing is that the child did actually live, so we can't just forget about it, we'd already given it a name.' I didn't ask him what that name was, so that I wouldn't have to remember it too. Years later, talking about something else entirely – but perhaps not thinking about that something else – he wrote to me: 'There is nothing more repellent than having to bury something that has only just been born.' He had still not separated from Eliane – or Eliane from him – when he spoke to me one day about a literary project of his that would require an experiment. He said: 'I'm going to write an essay on pain. I thought at first that I'd make it a strictly medical treatise and entitle it *Pain, Anaesthesia and Diathesis*, but I want to go beyond that. What really interests me about pain is its mystery, its ethical nature and how to describe it in words, all of which is easily within my grasp. I've decided that in a few days' time I'll stop taking the medication for my depression and see what happens, see how long I can bear it, and simply observe the process of my mental pain, which always ends up taking on various physical manifestations, the worst of which are the excruciating migraines. The term 'migraine' always seems to be taken rather lightly, doubtless because of that old joke about headaches and dissatisfied wives, but it actually describes one of the greatest sufferings known to man. There is a possibility that if I want to stop the experiment at some point, it might already be too late, but I can't not do this research.' Xavier Comella had continued to write – novels, poetry and an epistemology, as well as what he called 'night watches'. Of all this work, the only piece we'd finally managed to get accepted for publication, by the Madrid publishing house that had brought us together in the first place, was his novel *Vivisection*, a much longer book than the one I'd read. Nevertheless, owing to endless delays, it had still not seen the light of day, and he was now working on a translation of Burton's *Anatomy of Melancholy*, commissioned by the same publishing house, who had chosen him for the task partly because of his profession. He was, therefore, still an unpublished author and, from time to time, he would despair, decide that he wanted to remain unpublished and cancel contracts only to have them drawn up all over again at a later date. Fortunately, his publisher was a patient man, both kindly and prepared to take risks, a combination almost unknown in the publishing world. 'Aren't you curious to see your book in print?' I asked. 'Of course I am,' he replied, 'but I can't wait. Besides,' he added, with his usual precision, 'once I've finished the essay on pain, I'll have completed 60 per cent of my work.' I said: 'The day we met, you told me that without the medication you'd probably kill yourself and, if that happened, you'd only have completed 50 per cent, perhaps less, depending on the percentage you give your essay. And 50 per cent really isn't very much, is it?' He gave that delayed laugh of his and said, slipping into the oddly naive idiom he occasionally resorted to: 'Honestly, the things you come out with...' I didn't feel particularly worried, since I'd always believed that he was exaggerating when he described the more dramatic and spectacular incidents in his life.

Over the following months, his letters became even more austere than usual and his childish writing more of a hasty scribble. Only at the end of those letters would he add a few words about himself or his state of health or about how his experiment was going: 'At the present time, the maximum speed at which we are travelling towards the future remains insufficient and we grow old not with respect to the future but with respect to our past. My future perfect can't wait to arrive, my past perfect is unstoppable.' Or: 'I've always lived with the fear that one day I would have to fall silent, for good. As you see, my friend, I'm more of a coward than ever.' But shortly after that, he wrote: 'Every day I grow more invulnerable inside and more combustible outside.' And later on again: 'The most heroic quality in man is not perhaps to live or to die but to endure.' And in the letter following that: 'What will they think of us? What do we think of ourselves? What will you think of me? I don't want to know. But the questions provoke a slight feeling of depression. That's all.' 'As I said to you in the course of our conversation outside the Jardin du Luxembourg,' he said once, referring to the work he was about to embark upon, 'my way into the subject entails provoking a relapse into endogenous colic and when the meandering route followed by my first seventy commentaries leads you at last to the final one, you will understand the reason why, especially if you remember what I told you about the exceptional circumstances of my illness. This new descent into Hades is a touch foolish and I'd be the first to reproach myself with that, but why fish for tuna when you could be catching shark?' And later: 'I'm not ill *again*. It's a continuation of the same illness.' He had to abandon the experiment sooner than expected. He'd estimated that it would take six months to reach crisis point but, after only a month, he had to be hospitalized for two weeks, unable to carry on without his medication and still without enough material to start writing. I know that both his family and his doctors rebuked him sharply.

Shortly after this, he suffered a series of setbacks and changes in his life, although he informed me of them only gradually, doubtless out of a sense of tact. He only told me that he'd separated from Eliane some time after it had happened. He didn't explain anything to me outright but, during a conversation – this time in Madrid where he was on a visit to a brother who'd moved there – he implied that there were four reasons: the death of a child doesn't necessarily bring people together, it can also drive them apart if the face of the other is a constant reminder of the death of that child; the years of waiting for something concrete to happen – a book and its publication – can be shattered when the long-awaited event actually takes place; while anything that begins in childhood is never truly over, neither does it ever truly reach fulfilment; with regard to your own pain, you have no option but to put up with it, what you can't do is to expect us to watch while you inflict pain on yourself, because we will never accept it as necessary. The break-up of his marriage did not, of course, mean the end of his adoration: Xavier hoped that the divorce would take a long time and that Eliane would stay on in Paris, even though she'd been offered an excellent job as an interior designer in Montreal.

Later on, he told me that the inheritance or private income he lived on had dried up (perhaps his father had been diverting money from the family business but had now grown tired of doing so). Up until then, Xavier's only paid work had been his monumental translation of Burton's *Anatomy of Melancholy*, of which he had still not completed even 50 per cent; he had no concept of schedules nor, of course, of getting up early. However, he decided to return to his original, neglected profession and took the necessary steps to do so in Paris, which he still had no desire to leave as long as Eliane remained there. While he waited to be given French nationality and to have his qualifications validated, he had to work as a nurse and, subsequently, in a clinic ('men and women, old people and adolescents, like so much plumbing: I go there to arbitrate among the horrors and the trivia'). He almost joined Médecins du Monde or Médecins sans

Frontières, organizations that would have sent him off to Africa or to Central America for a while, with all expenses paid but with no salary, which would have meant returning with empty pockets. Now that he couldn't spend all his free time writing, the pace at which he was able to work towards his famous 100 per cent had slowed considerably. He didn't much like talking about Eliane, he preferred to talk about other women, young and not so young, among them my Italian friend to whom I'd introduced him some years before. According to his version of events, she'd been very cruel to him; according to her version, she'd simply acted in self-defence. It seems that after spending one night together, he'd left her house only to return a few hours later with his luggage, all set to move in. She threw him out in feminine high dudgeon. I listened to both versions and offered no opinion, merely regretting that it had happened.

He was now no longer an unpublished author but, as expected, his novel didn't sell in Spain and was reviewed almost nowhere. When I went to Paris we used to arrange to have supper or lunch at Balzar or at Lipp, and that didn't change, but now he allowed me to pay for him whereas before he'd always imposed the law of hospitality: you're a stranger and you're in my city. He still dressed well – I remember he often wore a particularly smart raincoat – as if that were something his breeding would not allow him to give up; it was, perhaps, the only characteristic he'd inherited from his father. Now, however, the colours he wore were not so splendidly coordinated, as if that had always been dependent on Eliane's exquisite taste in anything to do with adornment. He mentioned her only once in a letter: 'From the severed root with Eliane furious lightning shoots sprout forth, draining away half my life.' We didn't see each other for two years and when I saw him again after that time, his physical appearance had changed somewhat and, with his usual tact, he forewarned me: 'I'm not only worn out mentally, I'm also in terrible physical shape. A witness to this is the galloping alopecia that obliges me to wear a cap to protect me from the ill-tempered autumns we get in this part of the world.' He'd had to move to a largely North African quarter. On one of my trips to Paris, I phoned him but got no reply, although I knew he was in town. Thinking that perhaps his phone had been cut off, I caught the metro and arrived at his remote and unfamiliar new house, or rather, what turned out to be a room, tiny and sparsely furnished, a desolate final stopping place. But, in fact, all I remember of that scene was the look of happiness on his face when he opened the door to me. On his desk was a glass of wine.

Things improved for him somewhat while I was away, travelling in Italy. Xavier had at last found the perfect job for his purposes, although, accordingly, it earned him little money: he got a job as a locum in a hospital, working more or less only when he wanted or needed to. As long as he worked a certain minimum number of hours per month, he could then increase those hours depending on how energetic he was feeling and on how much money he needed and this allowed him to hurry impatiently on towards the completion of his literary work. I never really understood this impatience, bearing in mind that, since *Vivisection*, nothing else of his had been published. His novel *Hecate*, the book entitled *The Edgeless Sword*, his *Treatise on the Will*, the poems he sometimes sent me, none of these was ever successful in finding a publisher. I remember two lines from one of his 'night watches': 'The wakefulness of your geminate soul/ is the sleep which I mere body deny myself.' Whilst everything he wrote remained extremely obscure, it nevertheless had a certain verve. I read very little of what he was writing and he was still engaged on translating Burton's *Anatomy of Melancholy*.

One morning – by then we'd known each other for about

ten or eleven years – we were once again sitting on the covered terrace of a café in St-Germain. He'd acquired a certain nobility of appearance and had discovered a way of combing his thinning hair, which did not look thin so much as lighter in colour. He seemed in good spirits after the misfortunes of recent years and he told me about the enormous progress he'd made in his writing. He had, he said, borrowing my ironic tone, completed 83.5 per cent of his entire body of work. Then he put on his confidential face and grew more serious: he had only two texts to complete now, a novel to be entitled *Saturn* and the long-postponed essay on pain. Given the novel's technical complexities, he would leave that to last and he now felt strong enough to return to his experiment and again stop taking his medication. He thought that, this time, he'd be able to last out long enough and be able to start writing as soon as he'd learned whatever it was he needed to learn. 'Over the past few years working in my profession I've seen a lot of pain, I've even controlled it; I've both fought it and permitted it, according to what was in the patient's best interests; I've suppressed it completely with morphine, as well as with other medications and drugs that can't be found on the open market and to which only doctors have access. Many are as closely guarded as state secrets; what you can buy in pharmacies and dispensaries is only a tiny fraction of what's available, but there's a black market in everything. I've seen pain now, I've observed it, gauged it, measured it, but now it's my turn to suffer it again, and not only physical pain, which is commonplace enough, but psychic pain, the pain that makes the thinking brain want only to stop thinking, but it can't. I'm convinced that consciousness is the source of man's greatest suffering and there's no cure for it, no way to blunt it, the only end is death, though even that you can't be sure of.' This time I didn't try to dissuade him, not even in the oblique, jokey way I had when he first announced his intention of embarking on this personal research. We had too much respect for each other and so I just said: 'Well, keep me posted.'

I can't honestly say that he did, in that he didn't keep me informed of his progress or of his thoughts on the subject, perhaps because he could only talk about it indirectly, by describing feelings and symptoms and states of mind, which he didn't in the least mind discussing and so, in the letters I received in subsequent months – I was commuting between Madrid and Italy at the time – he never said much about what was happening to him or what he was thinking, his letters were even more laconic than usual, but he did sometimes let slip the occasional disquieting remark – explicit or enigmatic, confessional or cryptic, depending on the context. I've just today been re-reading some remarks of his that fall into the second category, remarks that usually came at the end of his letters, just before he signed off or even after that, in a postscript: 'Pain thought pleasure and future are the four numbers necessary for and sufficient to my interest.' 'Nothing sullies one more than an excess of modesty: pay up rather than be your own Shylock.' 'Let's just do our best not to fall off the back of the train.' 'If you don't desert the desert, the desert will desert you, not in the sense that it will leave you, but in the sense that it will make a desert of *you*.' 'Best wishes and don't let anyone have it easy. They might make you pay for it.' That's the sort of thing he wrote. There was more of a sense of continuity, even a kind of progress, in the first category of remarks: 'I don't feel like writing, I don't feel like working or travelling or thinking or even despairing,' he said and then, in the next letter: 'I read so as to give some semblance of being occupied.' Some time afterwards, I thought that perhaps he'd recovered slightly, for he spoke openly – for the first time – of the experiment on which he was engaged: 'As for my ethical experiment in endogenous pain, I'm still waiting for the explosion of the time bomb I set ticking at the beginning of summer, but I don't know the day or the hour it's due to go off. You see how things are, but don't waste too much time thinking about it, it's too pathetic to merit any deep consideration, and if there can be said to be something titanic about all this, the truth is that I feel more like a midget.' I don't know what I wrote in reply nor if I even asked him about it, for we forget what's in our own letters the moment we put them in the letter box, or even before that, while we're still licking the envelope and sealing it down. He continued to give me only the bare outlines of his inactivity: 'A bit of medicine, very little wielding of the pen, rather more withdrawal. Dead wet leaves.' I remembered that, on his first and failed attempt, he'd mentioned a period of six months as the time he would need to go without his medication in order to achieve what he was after, and so, with the arrival of winter, I expected that his time bomb would either explode or he'd have to stop the experiment, even if that meant being rushed into hospital again. But that season only contributed to a worsening of his suffering, which he nevertheless still judged to be insufficient: 'For two months now I've been more dead than alive. I don't write, don't read, don't listen, don't see. I hear the distant rumble of thunder but I don't know if the storm is approaching or moving off, whether it's in the future or in the past. I'll close now: the vulture is already pecking at my left hemisphere.' I assumed he was referring to the tormenting migraine.

Another two months passed by with hardly any news and, at the end of that time, I received a phone call in Madrid from Eliane. After their separation I'd lost all contact with her but I still couldn't manage to feel surprised, instead I immediately thought the worst. 'Xavier asked me to call you,' she said, and since there was no indication as to when that had happened, I wasn't sure whether he'd asked her to do so before he died or if he'd asked her that very moment, assuming he was still alive. 'He suffered a serious relapse and he's in hospital, possibly for some time, but he can't write to you for the moment and he didn't want you to worry too much. He's been very ill, but he's better now.' Her words were as acceptably conventional as one would expect in such a phone call, but I did manage to ask her two things, even though that meant obliging a memory, that is, someone who was a memory twice over, to speak: 'Did he try to kill himself?' 'No,' she replied, 'it wasn't that, but he has been very ill.' 'Are you going to go back to him?' 'No,' she replied, 'that's not possible.'

During the final two years of our friendship, we wrote and saw each other less frequently, I only went to Paris once and he never again visited Madrid. He often either neglected to answer my letters or took a long time to reply, and everything requires a certain rhythm. There are other things I could say about him, but I don't want to talk about them now, they're not things I actually experienced. The last time we saw each other was on a very brief trip I made to Paris. We had lunch at Balzar; he'd got a bit fatter – his chest had filled out – and it rather suited him. He smiled a lot like someone for whom going out to lunch is something of an event. He told me cautiously and briefly that, during our silence, he'd finally written his essay on pain. He said he felt sure it would be published, but said nothing about the text itself. Now he was working, continuously but with enormous difficulty, on his last book, *Saturn*. It all felt rather remote: for me, his life had become even more fragmentary, more spectral, as if, on the final pages of the defective book, there was now only punctuation, or as if I'd begun to feel that he too were merely a memory or some fictitious character. Although he was almost bald by then, his face was still handsome. I remember thinking that the veins on his forehead, even more prominent now, stood out like high relief. We said goodbye there, in rue des Écoles.

After that, I received only one letter and a telegram. The former I received after some months had passed and in it he said: 'I'm not writing because I've finally got something to say to you, but simply because time passes and every day leaves me with less to say. Nothing positive. A horrible winter, full of recesses filled by swirling whirlwinds. Sediment and chaos. A dematerializing silence from my publishers. Divorce from Eliane. And a feeling of nausea as regards any creative work. Last week was filled by a coagulating tedium. The night before last was even worse: I was woken by a scream, my own.' And the postscript said: 'So I will darken for only a little while longer this my ash-grey matter.'

I didn't feel particularly worried by this and I didn't bother to reply because in two weeks' time I would be going to Paris anyway. That was a little over two years ago. I'd already been in the city for three days, staying as usual with my Italian friend, and I still hadn't phoned Xavier, wanting to get my business in Paris over with first. On the third day I returned to the house of that Italian friend, the one who had been cruel to him or who had acted in self-defence, and she told me of his voluntary death the day before yesterday. This time he wasn't too young, this time he didn't miss; he was a doctor, he was precise; and he avoided all pain. Some days later, I managed to phone his mother, whom I never met. She told me that Xavier had completed *Saturn* two nights before the day he died (his 100 per cent: he had reached the end of his life when he reached the end of the page). He'd made two copies and had written three letters, which were found on the table next to a glass of wine: a letter to her, a letter to his unsuccessful agent and a letter to Eliane. In the letter to his mother he'd explained the whole ritual: he would read for a while, listen to a bit of music and drink some wine before going to bed. Over the phone she was unable to tell me what music he'd listened to or what he'd read, and I never asked her again, so as not to have to remember that as well. Of the more than one thousand pages of Burton's *Anatomy of Melancholy*, he'd translated only seven hundred – 72 per cent – and the rest still awaits someone to finish the task. I don't know what happened to his essay on pain.

The telegram I found on my return to Madrid. This is what it said: 'EVERYTHING GOOD GOES NOTHING GOES WELL EVERYTHING BAD COMES BACK YOURS XAVIER.'

Today I received a letter that reminded me of this friend. It was written by a woman unknown both to myself and to him.

FRANCE

Before

ANNIE SAUMONT

translated by Christine Donougher

Mist on the river. Like a ribbon of gauze. Through it you can see the water rippling. You can see currents forming. Gentle currents.

The water slowly makes its way to the sea.

But first the river flows alongside the meadow and other meadows, alongside vegetable gardens and then under a stone bridge with arches that are green with moss.

There are dragonflies in the air streaking through the blueness of a cool morning, at the dawn of their lives, a day for a human being. The men are not angry. The men are pleasant and cheerful, on leave from all toil for the span of a dragonfly's life.

When is the bird pecking at the grain scattered round the earthenware jars at the entrance to the corn loft going to have eaten its fill? Scarcely does it start to shiver and hop about than a breeze makes the ladder creak.

A breeze. Then stillness. The cloud above has gold in its lining.

That was before. It was Sunday. The grown-ups were back from church. Not having insisted on everyone getting up early to go with them. Now at about eleven Mama said, What lovely weather for a picnic. Danilo, help me pack the basket.

On the table there's bread and cheese. Fruit and slices of dried meat. Danilo, pass me the knife, Danilo, stop daydreaming, open the pot of lard, don't wipe your fingers on your trousers. Here, you can also give me – And we'll take –

Papa said, Let's see how strong you are, young man. And the basket was heavy with food and our hearts were light.

Walking along the riverbank, they hear some rustling in the underwood, a titter of ill-contained laughter, and some whispered words. Mama says, It's Wara with the long hair who lives in the grey house by the lock. Papa says, And he comes from the other side, it's Terzine, the tobacconist's son. Mama says, Let's move away from here. Quietly so as not to disturb them. Papa says, That would teach them to behave more correctly in public places. Mama protests, the riverbank isn't a public place. She's right, it's a realm that doesn't belong to anybody and yet everyone secretly owns. Mama says, Let's go a bit further, there's room for everybody in this country.

Danilo wouldn't mind going further but the basket's too heavy. Danilo frets and complains. Papa takes him under the armpits, lifts him very high, and sets him on his shoulders. Papa's big brown hand grips the handle of the basket. Mama says, Wait, I've lost my sandal.

It's Sunday. This is before. At school during the week Danilo sits next to Mirela who comes from across the river. One evening after school Danilo tells white-haired Moumcha, who's Mama's mother, he tells her, and he can't keep still – stop it, you're making me dizzy – that Terzine has his Wara, OK, and they kiss each other in secret, OK, so it's not surprising then if Danilo has his Mirela, that's life, that's normal. When they're a little older Danilo and Mirela will go and kiss on the riverbank. Just to think of it makes you feel hot all over, makes you feel scary. Moumcha says, Don't think about it, sit down and eat your soup. You'll have your pudding afterwards. No, not an apple from the orchard. Something special, a surprise. I knew it was, Moumcha, says Danilo; and he's so glad he's still a little boy.

Mama carries her sandals in her hand and walks barefoot through the meadow. Papa says how foolish. He says it's crawling with snakes.

Danilo can't believe that the snakes would dare to attack Mama's pretty foot on such a bright and cheerful morning. Danilo sings to himself and pulls Papa's hair. Ouch, says Papa, tomorrow I'm going to be like Poupcha, as bald as an egg.

Again, they hear the stifled laughter of another Wara in the tall grass beyond the copse, and the higher-pitched whistling of another Terzine who has now stood up. They watch him approach the riverbank and he shouts, Hey, for no reason, to nobody. To someone on the other side within hearing distance.

A clump of trees. A fragrant hedge. With the path rising to the bridge and at the end of the path, on a slight slope, a field of thick clover, and Mama declares, No need to look any further. Setting down both Danilo and the basket, Papa says, Soon I shan't be able to carry you on my back any more, you're nearly a man now. Mama has already spread out a big linen cloth in the shade of a bush.

That was before.

Before, when the sky was blue and the river quiet, when the picnic basket was well stocked and they emptied it in the knowledge that the following week they'd have what they needed to fill it again.

When Wara waited for Terzine and Terzine came over the bridge and Mama would smile. Look how much in love the pair of them are. Moumcha announced gaily that she hoped to live long enough to go and dance to the sound of the violins with all the young people in their Sunday best when the lock-keeper's daughter got married to the tobacconist's son.

One day – before – a Sunday, Papa said something that he certainly shouldn't have, because Mama got cross, with furrowed brow and thin lips; with thunder in her eyes. Ordinarily calm and gentle Mama. He said that on the other side it wasn't the same as here. They weren't the same people. Mama protested, What kind of nonsense is that? Didn't Poupcha's grandfather come from across the river, and also, from what she said, one of Moumcha's distant ancestors? Papa shrugged his shoulders. Papa said, Sure. He said, Yes.

But when there was the rally in the square in front of the church and those speeches were made accusing the people opposite of behaving like barbarians, Papa again said yes. Mama and Moumcha stayed at home. Papa had decided that none of this was really any of the women's concern. Poupcha stayed behind too, so as not to miss his little afternoon nap. Papa had given orders, And as for you, Danilo, now you get yourself into the vegetable garden and thin out the radish bed for me.

Danilo ate three radishes, then jumped over the fence and walked through the streets to the square. In the square he saw men getting themselves worked up, looking red-faced and furious. Papa was the reddest and most furious of all, shaking his fist in the direction of the people opposite.

Yet that was before.

When Terzine used to cross the river to come and see Wara. When Terzine was so eager to clasp Wara in his arms that he would race madly along the parapet. She would go towards him, meeting him half-way. Wara with her long legs, and still light on her feet, would run as fast as her young man or else it was Terzine that had chosen to slow down a bit, so as to place their meeting under the protection of the angel with outspread wings that stood midway across the bridge. And the two lovers destined to be married wrapped themselves in an endless embrace. Passers-by laughed. Passers-by passed by and lowered their eyes or looked elsewhere.

That was before.

*

The rally broke up everything. The words that were said split in two the country that had never really been divided by the river. Since there was a bridge. And people on the one side used to cultivate on the other wheat, friendships, love. The words of the rally were words of hatred and anger. Never used until now on either side, words that before were only to be found in books, and suddenly the words had been spoken, hurled, yelled, and everyone knew that nothing was the same as it had been.

Yet that was before.

Before the rifles appeared. And then the machine-guns. And the cannons. Before a shell levelled the fountain, and bullets pitted the walls and façades. Papa kept saying, I told you. Those people over there have always been savages.

Mama says that Papa has no right to make such remarks. That it's adding fat to the fire. Or fire to the fat, everyone's getting muddled. In word and mind. It's on account of the war that makes so much noise. There are empty desks in the classroom, the ones that belong to the children who came from across the river when the bridge wasn't yet under crossfire from the two sides. Mirela doesn't come to school any more. Danilo has told this to Mama, and that Mirela was his girlfriend. Mama says that Danilo will see her again, promise, when the war's over. Mama smiles but it looks like a smile that's meant only to hold back the tears. And any tears that come, she sniffs. Moumcha has her own little cry, while peeling the vegetables. And then she rubs her eyes with the tea-towel.

Mama says that Wara can't see Terzine any more. The soldiers aim at the bridge and the boats day and night, and Terzine and Wara now have to exchange signs from afar. At first they tried to shout endearments at each other so loudly it sounded as if they were quarrelling. Wara doesn't talk any more. Or sometimes her lips move but not the least sound comes out.

Danilo would like to tell Mirela that he's been fishing for tadpoles in the pools left by the rainstorm in the bottom of the quarry-pits, they're full of the little creatures. He catches some and puts them in a jar. When Mirela comes back the tadpoles will have grown into frogs. They'll make a frog-size ladder for them out of twigs. The frogs will bring the warm weather.

Tomorrow was to be their wedding-day. Terzine and Wara's. Mama said, Those two had better be married without delay. She said to Papa, What's to be done? Have you seen Wara's belly?

Moumcha is knitting, with her head bowed. Danilo goes up and asks, Has Papa seen Wara's belly? Moumcha frowns, and drops a stitch, she picks it up again and mutters, Don't ask silly questions.

Wara used to sing, while wringing the sheets at the wash-house by the river under the shelter among the reeds. Wara used to laugh. That was before.

The junipers smell like mint. No, says Mama, they have their own juniper smell, their own smell intensified by the warmth of June. Danilo is adamant, It smells like the mint that grows on the opposite riverbank. Moumcha has turned away and says that he's dreaming, that he's imagining things.

Wara doesn't do her laundry in the river any more. Neither she nor any of the other women on this side, nor the women who used to come across the bridge, behind a donkey loaded with bundles of washing, kneeling-box, and beetle. Mama tells Danilo, No walking by the river. Moumcha says, Don't wander off. I'll tell you a story. Poupcha clears his throat and sighs. Papa says, Those bastards opposite. Mama says, They were our friends.

Wara stares straight ahead of her. Wara becomes very peculiar, her face has shrunk above her big-bellied body. Wara never laughs at all now. At school there's still no one on the bench beside Danilo where Mirela used to sit. At home Danilo has taken the lid off the gherkin jar and let the frogs go free. Mama said that they would die if they were kept prisoner.

There are people that have died. The ones that tried to cross the river. There's a bridge over the river that serves no purpose any more. There are people lying in the grass and the mud along the riverbank. Dead bodies that the people living here and the people living over there will come and fetch during the night.

There's Wara's belly, covered with blood. Mama says that Wara came down the path to the river to shout across to Terzine that the baby was about to be born. And Terzine should be there to hold it in his hands and name it. Wara said the baby would be called Danilo. Like you, says Mama. Danilo, a name she liked. Terzine didn't answer. Wara stayed a little too long by the wash-house. A shell exploded among the junipers.

The place where Wara is buried with the baby still in her belly is at the bottom of the meadow where Mama lost her sandal one Sunday, when we went for a picnic. They had to be put there because shells keep pounding the cemetery, rupturing the ground, opening up the graves. Mama said, These are bad times for our country. Papa said, Tears won't change anything. Danilo asked when Mirela would come back, and Papa replied, When pigs fly, when the world grows honest, when the barber doesn't charge for a shave, when we've killed all the traitors. Mama shouted, Oh, aren't you ashamed of yourself! Then he calmed down and mumbled sullenly, Maybe one day. In a very long time.

Poupcha was asleep, seated at the table, with his forehead cupped in his hands. Moumcha put aside her knitting. She closed the window overlooking the river. She wiped her eyes on the white curtain.

GERMANY

The Babbling of the Gods

HENNING BOËTIUS

translated by Martin Chalmers

He takes the bird out of the cage and puts it on the back of his hand. He stares at it for a long time. The bird is trembling, and this trembling penetrates into his hand, enters his forearm, his upper arm, finally from there to his shoulder, passes along the nerve tracts into the whole body of the man, who is sitting up straight on a chair in the middle of the room, his knees bent and one foot in front of the other, as if he were just getting up.

'Fly!' he says, and his voice trembles too. 'Fly at last, go, away with you. And send Homer my greetings.'

He is almost shouting now. But the bird makes no move to fly away. It is tame.

Then the man feels a wave of anger welling up in himself. A wave such as he saw only recently at the sea shore. Green and glassy with a white edge of foam.

He picks up a pair of scissors which by chance are lying there. 'How far is chance really chance?' he thinks, 'chance, if it really is so, is nothing else but betrayal of the soul.'

This now cannot be true chance. It is feigned. So he has no choice: he takes the pair of scissors in his right hand, raises the index finger of his left hand, in which he is holding the bird, shoves it under the wing, pushes it up and cuts it off.

The bird throbs in his hand like a crazy heart. Blood drips from the wing stump, tiny ruby red pearls, which cling to the feathers.

He runs to the window, throws the creature out. 'The cat,'

he mutters, 'the cat will get you!' Then he begins to pack his trunk. He stuffs his best clothes, his novel *Hyperion* and the little casket with her letters into it. He keeps back only her last letter. He has already crushed it and smoothed it out again many times. Now he reads it once more, runs his eyes over the tear-stained words. He wants to save up his anger. Until he is with her. It must not turn to despair, not to disappointment, not to sadness, not to indifference.

'I am lonely, lonely and my life is running out like an hour glass.' They are his words, which she is writing to him. 'Damnable copyist,' he shouts. 'Can you not use your own words! Have you ever used words of your own at all? All your letters were the echo of my letters, a false imitation, which I took for the original.'

His nervous gaze becomes fixed on a fingernail-sized brown mark on the wallpaper. He crumples the letter into a ball, throws it at the animal, which disappears in a crack in the wall. 'Repulsive cockroach,' he says, 'this whole house is full of repulsive cockroaches, I too am a repulsive cockroach. I too should disappear into a crack in the wall.'

The warmth of the May day pours in through the window. He leans out of it, so far that he almost loses his balance. Now fall like the bird did. He sees: nothing is lying on the grass under the window, nothing on the blooming oleander bushes, the rhododendrons, the roses. 'The black beast has it,' he whispers, satisfied.

He stands at the window and holds his face to the sun. It is difficult to save up a rage for a long time. One must temper it. Not freeze it, but bake it. As one makes clay masks. First shape it, then into the oven with it!

He has closed his eyes, in order to see the red face, disfigured by pustules, of his beloved, in order to imagine the voice from her letter, which for a week he has read again and again, till he knows it by heart. 'I am lonely, lonely and my life is running out like an hour glass. My time is up. And what remains to me is only a noble end.'

'You shall have an ignoble end, not a noble one,' he hisses, 'you whore of your husband and of my language, yes, you carried on the same lecherous game with his abhorrent body as with the language of Homer. It was the same up and down for you, you harlot. Woe to you, if you really die now from the measles of your bastards, yes they are bastards, for your husband begat them although there was no love between you! Now you want to make free with death as well, want to surrender to him, so that he steals from me the beauty of inextinguishable longing! You are killing my life's plan, if you die, you shall suffer for that.'

From his twisted features he feels how terribly rage is etched in his face. This is the right moment to push the mask into the kiln.

He stands like that for a long time, petrified, but resembling no suffering Greek image of a god, no thirsting Tantalus say, whom the gods placed with stiff knee joints in a pond beneath a tree, whose fruit-laden branches rose when he reached up for them. Tantalus had the face of one tormented. He, however, is like a child slain by the basilisk gaze of the piercing sun.

The door of his room opens. A woman in a pale dress comes in, noiselessly, very beautiful, an Aphrodite, enjoying her late summer. It is the consul's wife. She holds a bag in her hand. 'Here, Hölderlin,' she says. 'Something for the long journey, something that will restore your body and your senses when you are exhausted from walking. Do you really not wish to take the mail coach?' Then she adds in a low voice: 'Or not sleep on your decision just once more?'

He does not turn round, turns his back on her. 'You too a Diotima,' he thinks. 'With you too it would be easy to tempt out the rapturous soul from the body like a butterfly and to leave to the husband the lifeless doll of the body! Whether

Frau Gontard from Frankfurt or Frau Meyer from Bordeaux, always the same game! Is it then my fate, to be the butterfly catcher in all these marriages?'

Only now does he turn round very slowly, like a figure on a toy clock which has almost wound down. When the consul's wife sees his face, she cries out. It is the face of a murderer at the moment of the crime.

As so often after an abrupt leavetaking he walks with heavy, very long strides away into the future, as he calls it. He does not step out, he stamps on the landscape lying before him with the tips of his boots as if it were an object that stands in the way of his future.

So it was as he set out for Bordeaux last winter, as in the snow-covered high Black Forest he went at the snow, which flew like dust, with his boots. So it was then, as after the quarrel with Susette's husband, he left the Gontard family.

In this violent walking his spirit leaps in ever new fragments from line to line, while his body carries the burden of the movement like a full sack. He listens to the rhythm of the verses, the babbling of the gods, only half intelligible to the mortal.

                    ways of the wanderer!
For   shadows of trees
And hills, sunny where
The path runs
Up to the church,
                    rain like showers of arrows,
And trees loom, drowsing, yet
Strides of the sun arrive.
For just as more hotly
It burns above the vapour of cities
So does the sun move above
The draped walls of the rain

For like ivy
Branchless the rain hangs down. But
More beautifully to travellers blossom the roads. . .*

When at evening a ferryman takes him across the Dordogne, his rage has almost evaporated. The ferryman has the face of a man who has grown old in dignity, it glows bronze-coloured in the evening light, Charon: an old, kindhearted man.

Hyperion the Titan, son of Uranus and Gaia, the Earth, father of the sun god, reaches into the bag and shares bread and wine with the ferryman. He has already forgotten what happened in Bordeaux, and with each dip of the oars the forgetfulness becomes deeper. How the gentle landscape resembles the Elysian fields of Greece, the ancient blessed shores! Is that not everything that we need to live? Friendship? A feeling of strangeness far from home which turns to true intimacy?

When they are at the opposite bank, he does not know whether he has arrived in Hades or returned to the living. He offers Charon the golden olive branch as the living do. The gift is returned. Then he opens his mouth, so that Charon can take the obolus from it, as is customary with the dead, in whose mouth a coin is placed as payment for the passage. Charon is not satisfied. He wants more, he wants a whole gulden; much too high a reward for the crossing of the Acheron. 'Times are bad,' says the old man with the stubbly beard. 'You are a stranger travelling by a roundabout route, you will have your reasons. Since the assassination attempt, the police do not like us to take across strangers who want to avoid the town.'

*This translation of the first few lines of *Griechenland* [Greece], first version, is taken from *Friedrich Hölderlin: Poems and Fragments*. Translated by Michael Hamburger. 3rd edition, Anvil Press (1994)

The assassination attempt two years ago, he thinks, the infernal machine of Paris, there were many dead, blood on the streets, the window cross bars, falling from heaven like rain. Screams, which do not cease circling above the deep wound in the earth. But it did not strike down the tyrant. Again hate seizes him and presses his tongue down into his throat like a gag. It is betrayal, betrayal of mankind, to want to rule.

For no one should rise up to be master, who is not a merciful god and loves the virtues of friendship.

He sits in the boat and chokes. At last he has the gag out. 'There,' he screams at the ferryman, 'take your dirty money and leave me in peace.' He runs on, drags his trunk along with him, jabs his boots angrily into the soft, yielding body of the dusk. Only when it is dark and he is afraid of losing his way does he look for an inn, drains the bottle of wine in his room, has a second brought, takes the letter in his hands again, smooths it, moves the candle closer and reads. It is his handwriting, she has forged it. 'Copyist,' he mutters. 'I am coming to reclaim the original.'

The following day he is calm. He strides out with firm, resolute steps. Helios, his son, has challenged him to a duel. They fight with glittering swords. Again and again he feels the burning blade pass through his brain. He is not wearing a hat, his hair is thin. Nothing protects him from Apollo's sword strokes. They strike his eyes, beat jangling sparks from his bones. Once as he stands still in the shade of a tree, in order to draw breath, he sees the sunlight run from his breeches, until he is standing in a dazzling pool.

He looks to the sky. In fact the sun is just as he last saw it as a child, a circular opening in the blue sky, from which a hot jet of liquid gold pours down.

A terrible suspicion springs up inside him. This is not at all the daytime in which men live, it is the eternal night of Hades. Only the sensitivity of his eyes makes everything appear so bright in the little illumination that penetrates the round opening in the heavens.

He walks on, hour after hour, the effort makes his eyes protrude, swells the veins on his forehead. Sweat pours down his body, his feet bleed. Yet he finds the walking so easy that he does not feel his wounded feet, nor the dryness of his throat. For this time he has a true goal.

At other times he has mostly gone away from something, from calamity, from weariness, from hopelessness. This time he is moving towards a goal.

Ten days later he arrives in Paris. He has never seen such a large city. Very many souls must have strayed here. The thought that they perhaps lived here of their own free will seems strange to him.

He seeks the rue Saint-Nicaise, the scene of the assassination attempt. It is a narrow alley. The marks of the explosion can still be seen everywhere. It is true the crater has been filled up and the pavement repaired, but the houses have not yet been rebuilt. Cracks in the masonry, gaping windows, skeletal roof timbers whose covering has been blown off.

He stands there for a long time and stares at the devastation, until he is addressed.

'It is dangerous, sir, to stop in this place so long. There are informers everywhere. The delinquents have not yet been found. It is believed that they were foreign Jacobins.' The stranger grips him by the arm.

'Come, down here to the wine cellar. You look as if you had drunk too much sun in recent days.'

He allows himself to be drawn into the cool darkness of a subterranean tavern. Then they sit in front of two jugs of wine and talk in German. 'I come from Mainz,' says the other. 'I am one of the crazy men, who came here during the Revolution, in the hope of a new beginning to human history. Now we have a new calendar, but men have remained as they were. That's how it is with ideals. They are figments of the imagination. One destroys them, if one comes too close to them. It is as if a rough hand were to snatch at a spider's web to rescue the dead fly in it. Who are you, friend?'

'I am Fritz from Nürtingen in Swabia. I have been a private tutor in Bordeaux.'

'Why did you take a look at the place? You need have no fear of me. I am not one of Fouché's creatures. You can trust me.'

The word trust, with its soft cat's fur over the vowel, seems so amusing to Hölderlin, that he suddenly has to laugh. He laughs like a little boy. The other laughs too. Then they drink to one another.

'I wanted to see, if there is a hole there, through which one can get out. Somewhere, after all, there must be a way out of this prison. One can perhaps blast one's way to freedom!'

'My dear Fritz. The only human who perhaps got out through the hole that day, so thoroughly, that not even a snippet of her was ever found, seems to be that little street walker, who was passing by chance and was hired by the assassins, for a derisory fifteen sous, to hold tight the reins of the nag with the cart on which the powder barrel stood.'

'Did you say "snippet"? I perceive the poet in you. But tell me now, why did this mad tyrant escape?'

Hölderlin feels the blood throbbing in his temples. His hand tightens round the wine glass.

'He owes his life to his wife's vanity. She wanted to go to the Opera, he did not, for he was tired. They quarrelled, she triumphed, she took a long time in front of the mirror to drape her Egyptian shawl to advantage, they were late, the coachman was drunk, drove too fast, in other words, so many circumstances which upset the assassins' calculations. One must conduct marriages, in order to be proof against the great catastrophes. I sense that you lack this protection. You are unmarried, and moreover unhappily in love. People in your situation always look a little like birds in winter, feathers ruffled in order not to lose too much warmth.'

'I love a married woman. She is as beautiful as Aphrodite.'

'Why do you not elope with her?'

'She has four children, I have no profession, other than that of pastor, which I cannot practise because it requires the greatest skill at lying. I am a poet, a calling which, as you surely know, presumes the art of honesty. We have parted for ever. She required of me, on taking leave, that I henceforth wholly live my language. I must not allow myself to be deformed by the all too coarse conditions of life. Must entirely listen to my inner voice, to capture it for her.'

'And? What came of it?'

'Rhythm. Everything is rhythm, babbling of the gods. That is why I compose my verses on the road, as I walk. Sometimes I hobble, sometimes skip.

'I also wrote a novel, before I found my beloved. When we met, we only needed to live what had already been written. I was private tutor to her children. For a long time her husband noticed nothing. But then the inevitable happened, jealousy, insults. I had to go. The man was demented.

'I wrote the novel once again, at greater length, with greater melancholy, evoked in it our separate lives as the most intense form of passion. And she, Diotima, swore eternal faithfulness to me in her thoughts. Now we could go on inventing ourselves, as children of hope, who know how to play out their brief eternities everywhere, provided that they are allowed to think of one another across every distance. We wrote each other letters. That now became our form of adultery. In her last letter she informed me that she was going to die. Of a children's sickness. It verges on betrayal.'

'You seem to be the Swabian Hamlet.'

'Rather the Swabian Ophelia.'

They laugh. This could be my friend, thinks Hölderlin. My Bellarmine.

'I expect a few old friends here in Paris. Can you tell me where I can meet them? You know them for sure, Heracles, Hermes, Aphrodite, Hera.'

Later, as he stands before the collection of antiquities in the Louvre, he sees that all the sculptures have cracks, cracks which are expanding further and further. He hears a groaning, the rage roaring deep inside the figures, which threatens to burst the marble asunder. The cracks grow ever wider, white lumps of rock fall off, noses, eyes, ears shatter, until the black mask, which lay hidden behind each noble head, bursts forth.

On the 7th of June he arrives in Strasbourg. He dispatches the trunk to Nürtingen to his mother's address. Then he walks downstream towards Frankfurt. Again and again he throws sticks into the water and tries to keep pace with the current. On the 11th of June he is in Frankfurt.

He knows the huge house on the Grosser Hirschgraben inside out. After all he and Susette explored every corner, chamber, hiding place for the brief meetings, the passionate embraces, the hurried games of love. It is a labyrinth of splendid and shabby rooms, long passageways, pantries and boudoirs. He finds his way here like a sleepwalker. He needs no thread of Ariadne. He knows exactly where to find her, in her bedroom, which is separate from that of her husband, deep in the heart of this maze. Covered in shame, they again and again committed adultery there. It seemed to them a place especially safe from unexpected visitors. Now he would even find the room in the dark, for he catches a sharp smell of camphor.

At her door he sees a servant whom he knows. 'It is good that you have come,' says the old man. 'She has often asked for you of late.'

'Not a word,' says Hölderlin and puts a finger to his lips.

'I am Orpheus, come to fetch his wife. If you tell anyone, you will meet a terrible end. I shall take you with me to the Hyperboreans to the end of the world. There you must be happy for ever.'

He seizes the old man by the collar and shakes him, full of rage at the old, weak flesh. The servant nods, he believes everything that this strange man foretells for him.

He opens the door to her room and goes in, feeling, as he does so, that he is plunging into a mirror. Then he sees her in the alcove. She lies in the cushions as if laid out, as if already made ready for the visits of condolence. A candle burns beside the bed, although enough thin rays of sunshine penetrate the half closed shutters.

He comes slowly closer, does not walk, glides over like a shadow rather. She stares at the ceiling of the alcove, on which cherubs are painted, does not notice him. The candle flame lends her shining eyes a brightness, which does not seem to be of this world.

'Diotima,' he whispers. He opens his arms, spreads them wide. Then he sees the reddened face, disfigured by the scarlet fever, the swollen skin, the rash.

He bends over her, her gaze remains fixed, yet he knows that she recognizes him. 'Do you still love me?' he says. She tries to speak, but only a babbling comes from her mouth, a word which sounds like 'pallaksh'. Her neck is swollen, the raspberry red tongue unnaturally thickened. He feels pity. His anger is somewhere in the darkened room, but it is no longer in him.

Then he sees the jug of water beside her bed, the empty glass on the little table. It reminds him of the time in his childhood when he had scarlet fever. His mother had neglected to replenish the glass and for hours he had almost perished with thirst. He feels the rage return, feels it slip into his hands. When he puts them around her neck, he feels the heat of the fever and the frantic pulse in her arteries. 'Infect me, so that at least something of you remains,' he says. He bends down and kisses her lips.

He takes the jug and pours water into the glass. Then he pushes his arm under her neck and lifts her a little, puts the glass to her lips, presses the thick tongue to the side with his finger, pours some of the fluid into her mouth. Finally he carefully puts her down again. It seems to him as if the expression in her eyes has changed, as if a little of the fear of death has gone from them.

He stands up and goes to the door. There he turns round once more. 'I needed a living ideal,' he says. 'There are no dead ideals. With you my language will die. If you do not regain your health, Susette, I shall never again utter your name. I shall also no longer write. Your life is the book in which I wrote all my lines.'

He whispers, for he does not want to torment her with his words. Then he walks down the passageways with a firm step, like a soldier, head held high, his sunburnt face no longer bowed before a secret disgrace.

Outside in the brightness he takes long strides again. This time going south towards home. Now only his mother is there. At least he can be sure that she does not understand him.

On the evening of the very same day he reaches Darmstadt. He sleeps in a barn at the edge of town. During the night he is robbed. All his money, more than seventy Flemish guldens, is taken from him. He does not defend himself. He laughs, while one of the robbers holds him fast. Then he goes on. Not as fast as before any more, for the anger has vanished for the present.

On the 30th of June Hölderlin arrives in Stuttgart. 'Matthison,' he says. 'I am here Matthison. Matthison I am here. Matthison not a word about the matter. I am here Matthison, Matthison not a word.'

Later his friend Matthison reports that he looked as pale as a corpse, with hollow, wild eyes, long hair and beard and dressed like a beggar.

He stays with his friend Landauer. Here a letter reaches him at the beginning of July with the news of Susette's death. As he reads it, his eyes fill with tears, in which the words become blurred. Then he nods, again and again, like a man full of the most profound approval of a happening which does not directly concern him, but of whose rightness he is nevertheless convinced.

'Pallaksh,' he says and nods again. His friend Landauer, with whom he is staying, tries to comfort him. 'Pallaksh,' says Hölderlin and nods.

Landauer does not understand what the word means. He is unaware that it means 'Yes,' but also 'No' in the language of the gods.

Hölderlin walks to Nürtingen to his mother. He moves more hesitantly than usual, sometimes makes detours, slinks quietly through the wood.

When he is standing in front of the house, his mother is just opening a shutter on the first floor. 'Come up here immediately,' she calls, 'I have something to say to you.'

'Pallaksh,' says her son and makes haste.

Leaning against a wall stands a beautiful, slim woman with a severe expression, a stiff figure in a black dress, widowed twice over. She holds letters in her hand. In front of her on the floor an empty, opened trunk. 'You have sinned, Fritz.' At first he does not understand. His glances are restless, like a captured bird. Her thin neck tightens, the larynx bounces up and down with each injured word. 'You have committed the sin of the flesh with a married woman.'

Then he sees, as he sits in front of her with drooping shoulders on a stool, his mother change, sees the bristles on her face sprout. Both fathers rise up in the woman, his own father, who died when little Fritz was two years old, and the stepfather, who died when Fritz was nine. Mother parricide, now it is his turn. Fear chokes him. He hears a roaring inside himself, a river in spate which surges muddily between low banks which have been half flooded. He looks at the woman who is reproaching him for having sinned with a married woman. His gaze is filled with a fearful lust to kill.

Then he begins to laugh, finally to scream. There it is again, the hot sun of anger. It bursts forth from this hole in the twilight. The raging current overturns the skiff, hurls the ferryman into the muddy flood, washes away the cries, the deadly fear, tosses him up in its eddy.

In blind murderous insanity Hölderlin chases his mother and everyone else out of the house, smashes the furniture, begins to throw the debris out of the window.

Three strong lads subdue the madman. He is brought, bound, to District Physician Planck.

When he addresses Planck as Charon, the latter has an idea. He has his fourteen-year-old son fetched. He is to read to the patient from Homer. The effect is astonishing. Hölderlin's features relax. He nods his head a couple of times. Later his bonds are removed. Each time a new fit threatens, the boy has to come.

So it goes on for a while with Magister Hölderlin, on into the night. Never again does he mention the name Susette Gontard, never again.

He is looked after. The attempt to heal him with the usual methods of the doctors, muzzling him with the pear-shaped gag, placing him under a jet of ice cold water, which breaks his scalp open, fails. Again and again Hölderlin begins to rave in blind rage. Between the fits he talks confusedly. An ocean of babbling, in which expressions of courtesy float like ships. Only when the brown leather mask is put on him, which fits the face like a second skin, leaving open only slits for the eyes, does he grow calm, so calm, that the doctor orders an examination, to see whether his patient is still alive. He has the mask removed and puts his ear to Hölderlin's mouth.

Hölderlin holds his breath, longer than a man has ever held his breath. Furrows of anxiety appear on the doctor's forehead. Then Hölderlin laughs. Shrill and wheezing, he laughs and laughs and the doctor recoils in fright and holds his deafened ear.

Finally Hölderlin is placed under the care of a master carpenter in Tübingen. He spends thirty-six years in a room in a tower. Exactly half of his life.

He calls himself Scardanelli, plays for hours on a piano, long formless soundscapes, in which he goes walking with a smile, sometimes for days on end without pause. Now his rage only rarely comes to visit. Since he no longer needs it, he plays with it like a child with a little wooden horse. Only if the name Hölderlin or that of Susette Gontard is mentioned in his presence does the old fury burst forth. Now and then he composes verses with childish rhymes. He regularly writes short letters to his mother, which consist of twisted expressions of courtesy. They are little boxes which contain the emptiness of infinite hate.

AFTERWORD

In Hölderlin's otherwise well documented biography there is a gap of seven weeks. It concerns the period of time between the 10th of May 1802, when Hölderlin, to all appearances unexpectedly, left his post as tutor with the Hamburg consul in Bordeaux, and his arrival in Stuttgart around the 30th of June. Only the date when he crossed the border at Strasbourg, on the 7th of June, is known. What happened on the journey, whether, for example, he went on foot as usual, is unknown. Above all, it seems surprising that he should have taken three weeks to reach his home in Swabia from Kehl, near Strasbourg.

The gap would be less interesting if two factors of decisive importance to his life did not fall within this space of time: the death of his great love Susette Gontard on 22 June in Frankfurt and the evident breakdown of his psychic identity. Much to the irritation of his colleagues, the French Hölderlin scholar Pierre Bertaux has seen an obvious connection between the two events. Bertaux suspects that Susette Gontard, Hölderlin's Diotima, informed her distant lover by post of her illness and that he set off impetuously to see her just once more. The three weeks after he crossed the border leave sufficient time for Hölderlin to visit Frankfurt secretly.

This story is an imagined reconstruction of those seven weeks.

NORWAY

The Invisible Ones

KJELL ASKILDSEN

translated by Anne Born

When Bernhard L. went back to his childhood home for his father's funeral Marion gave him a rather clumsy hug. It was a hot afternoon and she had big wet patches under her arms. 'You've come then,' she said. He said he was tired after the journey and would like to change. She had prepared the attic room for him. The window was open and the floor was flooded with sunshine. He took off all his clothes and lay down on the bed. He took hold of himself and tried to conjure up the fantasies that had excited him so much in the narrow compartment of the train, but was unable to. Then he heard Marion coming upstairs and got dressed again. Sounds from the street outside came in through the window. Marion went downstairs again. He opened the wardrobe door and hung up his black suit.

When he went downstairs to Marion a little later she sat in the living room crying. He thought she hadn't heard him come in, but he wasn't sure, for she looked as if he had surprised her doing something wrong. He didn't know what to say. He walked across to the window. He stood looking out at the small back garden. 'You were fond of him,' he said. A black cat jumped on to the wooden fence. 'I should have been nicer to him,' she said. 'But you were the one who looked after him,' he said. The cat jumped down from the fence and up on to the roof of the old bicycle shed. She said: 'He could be so. . .but then he had a lot of pain. . .sometimes I almost wished. . .I feel such remorse.' He lit a cigarette. 'I didn't think he was going to die,' she said. He asked how it had happened. She paused for a while before she replied. He knocked off his ash into the single plant pot. 'He was sitting in that chair,' she said. 'I was in the kitchen. He asked me to come and read the newspaper to him. I said I was busy getting dinner. He said he wasn't hungry. But I am, I said. It was quiet for a while, then he said: Are you coming soon? I didn't answer, he irritated me. A bit later he called my name, or said it, he didn't shout. But I didn't come in for two or three minutes, and then he was dead.'

Bernhard pictured his father, but he didn't feel anything. Marion started to weep again. He looked around for an ashtray to stub out his cigarette in. He went into the kitchen and threw the cigarette into the bin. Then he drank a glass of water. The doorbell rang. Marion asked him to open the door. It was a woman. She looked at him and said: 'You must be Marion's brother.' 'Yes,' he said. She went into the living room in front of him. Marion wasn't there, he thought she must have gone out to the kitchen to dry her eyes. The woman gave him her hand, it was damp, but he took no notice. 'Camilla,' she said. 'Bernhard,' he said, 'I'll go and find Marion.' At that moment she came in. He stood and looked at them for a moment; they were so totally different he couldn't understand what they had to do with each other. Camilla stood with her back to him, her clothes were close fitting, he thought: Doesn't Marion realize she is just being used? The next moment he pushed the thought away. Camilla turned towards him and said something. He answered. She smiled and lowered her eyes. She works in a shop, he thought. Marion uttered half a sentence and went out to the kitchen. He opened a window. 'Sit down,' he said. She did so. 'I'm sure Marion is glad to see you,' he said. He laughed. He sat down opposite her. He asked if she had known his father. She started on a long explanation, looking at her hands and at him by turns: she had known him and yet not known him. She sat on the edge of her chair with her knees together and her crossed hands in her lap. He offered her a cigarette and lit it for her. He wondered which of them would discover first there was no ashtray. At last he said: 'I'll go and find an ashtray.' He went out to the kitchen. Marion was making open sandwiches. She gave him a very small ashtray. 'Haven't you got a bigger one?' he asked. She clicked her tongue and gave him a big one. He went into the living room. He asked Camilla how she and Marion had met. She told him. Marion came in and spread a white cloth on the table. 'Let me help you,' said Camilla, but she didn't get up. 'No, there's no need,' said Marion. She laid the table and they ate. Camilla and Marion talked about a woman friend who had given birth to a child with a hole in its back. It was seven o'clock. Bernhard noticed that Camilla kept looking at him. He sat considering her. Then a wasp appeared and landed on one of the sandwiches and Camilla got up and went into the middle of the room. She said she was allergic to wasp stings. Marion picked up a cheese sandwich and slapped it down on the slice of bread where the wasp was. Bernhard laughed. Marion went over to the window and threw both pieces of bread into the back garden. 'There,' she said. Bernhard laughed again. Marion and Camilla sat down. 'Eat now,' said Marion. Bernhard thought she looked happy. Camilla said the last time she was stung she had to go to the doctor. 'Eat up now, Bernhard,' Marion said. He said he'd had enough. He rose. He went out into the hall and upstairs. The door of Marion's room was shut, he opened it and stood on the threshold looking in. The bed was unmade and clothes were thrown over the chairbacks. A large framed photograph was on the chest of drawers: their father and mother on the steep flight of steps to the street, they were smiling. He closed the door and went downstairs again.

A little later Camilla got up to go. Bernhard went up to the attic. When he leaned out of the window he could look down at the steps to the street just below him. Camilla stood facing the door; he could just see her hair and a bit of her body. Marion was talking but he couldn't get what she said. 'No, no, not at all,' and Camilla. She began to go down the steps. He pulled his head in. He saw her cross the street and disappear down the alleyway between the watchmaker's and the baker's. 'Bitch,' he said to himself. He met his eyes in the mirror above the chest of drawers, held them a while, quite a long time, his eyes began to smile and he said: 'That's it. Bitch.'

He kicked off his shoes and flopped on to the bed, but rose again straight away, went over to the door, bent down to find out what he could see through the keyhole. He saw the top of the stairs and the door to what had been his parents' bedroom. He lay down again. Hardly any noise came in through the window, just the sound of a car going by. It was ten minutes to eight. He thought: I must ask for an extra pillow. He lit a cigarette. There wasn't an ashtray. He put one of his shoes on the bedside table, sole up. I suppose I ought to go down to her, he thought. After all, it's for her sake I came. I'll have to ask her for an extra pillow, and an ashtray. Perhaps she's sitting waiting for me. Perhaps she thinks she can't go out because I've come. He knocked off his ash on the sole. He tried to think of something they could talk about. Then he heard a door closing, followed by steps on the stairs. He hurried over to the door and put his eye to the keyhole. He saw her clearly as she crossed his field of vision, he saw her turn her head and look straight at him.

A little later he went down. He walked quietly.

He went out into the garden and sat down on a green folding chair beside a round wrought-iron table. In a while he noticed the stillness: nothing moved and no sound could be heard. He felt suddenly abandoned, almost as if he was imprisoned, and stood up. He walked between the narrow flowerbed and still narrower kitchen garden, over to the wooden fence. He stood with his back to the fence looking at the house and thought: but there's nothing for me to do here. At that moment he saw Marion; she was in the living room, some way from the window; she looked at him. She can't be sure I saw her, he thought, and turned his gaze. Then he squatted down and busied himself weeding the radishes while glancing at the door. She didn't appear. She must think I didn't see her, he thought. He went on weeding, and a feeling of satisfaction gradually spread through him, almost a kind of happiness, watching the clean and orderly miniature landscape emerging from his handiwork. He stopped peeking at the door, she could come if she liked, he was busy, he had a whole kitchen garden to do.

He had reached the lettuces when Marion came out with a man with a bottle in his hand. Marion carried three glasses. Bernhard straightened his back. Marion introduced him, the man was called Oskar. She put the glasses on the round table. Bernhard nodded to Oskar, then he went to rinse his hands under the garden hose. He felt trapped. Marion poured out the wine. Bernhard shook the water from his fingers and went over to the table. Oskar put out his hand. 'I'm wet,' said Bernhard. 'Doesn't matter,' said Oskar. He's a driver, thought Bernhard. 'Skål,' said Marion. They drank. Oskar took off his jacket, his arms were covered with curly black hair. 'Oskar and I are getting married,' said Marion. 'Congratulations,' said Bernhard. He tried to imagine them but couldn't. 'Oskar is in the police force,' said Marion. 'Is he now,' said Bernhard. Father died at a convenient moment, then, thought Bernhard. He looked at Oskar and said: 'This is the first time I've had a drink with a policeman.' 'Isn't it a lovely evening,' said Marion. 'Your vegetables need watering,' said Bernhard. 'Oh, well,' said Marion. 'They say the fine weather's going to last,' said Oskar. 'I'll water them,' said Bernhard. They drank. Bernhard smoked. Oskar talked about a colleague who had had his canoe stolen. Bernhard finished his wine and Marion refilled his glass. He rose and went into the house, up to the top and into the attic. He stood there and waited for a while, then he went down again. He sat down and took a big gulp of wine. He lit a cigarette. Marion and Oskar were talking. I must remember to ask for an extra pillow, thought Bernhard. Then he thought: I'm not going to the funeral. He said it to himself again, several times. Marion rose. 'I'm just going to –,' she said. 'Do you think I could have an extra pillow?' said Bernhard. 'Yes, of course.' She went into the house. Oskar scratched his arm. 'Have you known each other long?' said Bernhard. 'Eight months,' said Oskar. 'So you knew my father?' 'Yes.' 'Well?' 'No, not well. He was ill, as you know. He didn't really feel like seeing anyone except Marion. Oh, and you, of course.' Bernhard laughed. 'Me,' he said. Marion came out again, she had a jacket over her shoulders. Bernhard stood up. He went over to the old bicycle shed; there had been a watering can there at one time. It was still there. He filled it from the hose and went across to the kitchen garden. He couldn't hear what Marion and Oskar were saying. The earth round the radishes grew black. He thought: I'm sure he's a brute. And suddenly his fantasies from the train came back to him, very clearly, and Camilla came into the picture and took the place of the anonymous woman. He wanted to take the fantasy up to the attic with him, and went to put away the watering can in the shed. Marion said: 'We ought to have a chat tomorrow, Bernhard.' 'Tomorrow?' 'Yes, I've invited some people back after the funeral, I hope you think that's the right thing.' 'Yes,' said Bernhard, 'I'm sure that's what usually happens.' He went on over to the shed, put away the can, lit a cigarette, went back to the table, sat down. Marion and Oskar went on talking. His wine glass was full, he drank. It had grown darker, their faces were not quite distinct, he felt almost unseen. Almost free.

A little later Marion and Oskar went in. Bernhard sat on,

smoking and sipping his wine. He thought: what a good darkness. Suddenly he felt a light pressure against his right leg, he jumped and cried out. The wine glass in his hand slopped over, and even though almost at the same moment he saw it was a cat that had brushed against his trouser leg, the sharp fear took hold again, like a humiliation, and he kicked out at the cat and felt his foot connect. He pushed his chair back and stood up, stayed stock still for a moment, then tore himself free and began to walk to and fro on the paved path in front of the house. He repeated his own name to himself, time after time, like an exorcism, and gradually grew calmer. He stopped under the open living room window, listened for voices, but all was quiet. He went over to the north side of the house, to the gate opening on to the street, lifted the big latch and went out. He crossed the street and entered the alleyway between the watchmaker's and the baker's, stopped there and ran his eyes along the old houses that leaned against each other. Then he turned and went back the same way. Bitch, he said to himself, bitch, bitch, bitch. He went through the gateway. He lit a cigarette. Music came from an open window of the house next door. He dropped the half-smoked cigarette and trod on it and thought: I must remember ashtrays. He walked through the living room and into the kitchen. Marion was ironing a white blouse. He was afraid she might want to talk, so he said he was tired and wanted to go to bed. She looked at him and smiled. 'You're not feeling very well, are you?' she said. 'I'm all right,' he said, 'just tired.' He asked for an ashtray. She found one for him and said she had put an extra pillow on his bed. He touched her underarm with his index finger, and she looked at him, almost pleadingly, he thought. Then he said goodnight and went upstairs.

Next day at the funeral he sat between Marion and their father's nephew Gustav. Marion held a handkerchief in her hand but she didn't use it. The minister talked about a dutiful father and the sorrow and loss of the bereaved, which time might lessen but could never wholly take away, for such were the ties of blood and the law of love. When the notes of the final hymn faded away Bernhard quickly left the chapel and went out into the street. He lit a cigarette. There were only three left in the packet, and he thought: I must remember to buy some more. After a while Marion appeared with Oskar and Camilla. Bernhard looked the other way. He thought of how he had taken Camilla in the attic the night before: she had resisted but he had conquered her. He started to cross the street. Marion called to him. He stopped and turned round. 'You can ride with Camilla,' she said. 'I must get some cigarettes,' he said, 'I'll take a taxi.' She looked at him. 'As you like,' she said. He laughed. 'What's the matter,' she said. 'Nothing,' he said. He went on along the pavement. As you like, he said to himself. As you like, as you like. He stopped at a news stand and bought two packets of cigarettes, then hailed a taxi. The driver looked at him in the mirror and after a moment he said: 'Midweek celebration?' 'Yes,' he said. 'Wedding?' 'Yes, my sister's getting married.' 'Fun and games then, eh?' 'Yes, fun and games.' Bernhard moved close to the door so the driver's eyes vanished from the mirror. He took off his black tie and put it in his pocket, then unbuttoned the top button of his shirt. 'You may as well stop here,' he said. 'I have to get some cigarettes. I'll walk the rest of the way.' He paid the driver, who told him to enjoy himself. Bernhard laughed. 'Thanks,' he said.

The guests had arrived. Some of them went up to Bernhard, introduced themselves and made their condolences. They spoke in hushed voices and looked concerned. Bernhard lit a cigarette. Marion smiled at him. Then she asked everyone to sit down. Bernhard sat at the smallest table. Charlotte, his mother's sister, sat beside him. 'I'd like to sit next to you,' she said. 'Would you?' he said. Marion and Camilla poured out coffee. There were ashtrays on the table, he stubbed out his cigarette. ‘Ah, well,’ said Charlotte. Bernhard offered her the plate of sandwiches. ‘Ah, smoked salmon,’ she said, ‘it’s my favourite.’ ‘Take two,’ said Bernhard. Camilla came and sat down opposite him. ‘May I really?’ said Charlotte. ‘Of course,’ said Bernhard. ‘I will then,’ she said. She snickered. ‘We should take what we want,’ said Bernhard and put the plate in front of Camilla. He looked at her, met her eyes, she smiled. He thought: If you only knew. They went on eating. ‘Did you know, Bernhard,’ said Charlotte, ‘now I’m the eldest in the family.’ ‘Are you,’ said Bernhard. ‘So next time it’s my turn,’ she said. ‘You can’t be sure of that,’ he said. ‘Oh, I think so,’ she said. He didn’t reply. Charlotte put her hand on his arm. ‘It doesn’t matter, you know,’ she said. ‘Doesn’t it,’ he said. He looked around him. No one looked troubled any more. He passed the plate to Charlotte. ‘This is my fourth funeral this year,’ she said. ‘If you include my budgies.’ Bernhard laughed. ‘Budgies?’ he said. ‘Yes, they died two months ago. They were a male and a female, and they had eggs, and then they ate their children, and then they died.’ ‘Of eating eggs?’ said Bernhard. ‘I assume so,’ she said. ‘It’s against nature to eat your own children.’ Bernhard laughed. ‘Perhaps they were related,’ he said. ‘Who?’ she said. ‘The two budgies,’ he said. ‘Why?’ she said. ‘Oh, nothing,’ he said. He thought he felt Camilla looking at him and turned his eyes to her, so quickly that she didn’t manage to look away. He smiled and she smiled back. Next time I’ll look at her breasts, he thought. Marion stood up and tapped her cup with a spoon. She said she wasn’t going to make a speech but just thank them all for wanting to come and pay their respects to her father’s memory. She didn’t want to say anything about how she was feeling on such a day because that would only make her cry. She would just say thank you to everyone and she hoped they enjoyed the simple meal. Then she sat down, and the guests were silent for a few seconds, most with bent heads. Then they went on eating.

'What a nice little speech,' said Charlotte. 'Aren't you going to say something too?' 'No,' he said so sharply and loudly that both Charlotte and Camilla looked at him. He felt his face grow rigid. He crushed out his half-smoked cigarette in the ashtray. Charlotte put her hand on his arm, he pulled it away. He lit another cigarette. He said his name to himself, several times. Camilla sat bolt upright and stared at her plate. 'Well, well,' said Charlotte. Bernhard searched vainly for something to say. He grabbed the plate and passed it to Charlotte. 'No, thank you, Bernhard,' she said, 'I've had enough.' She said it so kindly and gently that he felt a wave of emotion. And suddenly he remembered a thing he had often heard her say when he was a boy, and he turned to her and said: 'Do you remember. . .there was a saying, a kind of rule you used to quote when I was small and you wanted to comfort me, it began with sigh heart. . .do you remember?' Charlotte smiled. 'Oh, yes, I remember. Sigh heart, but break not, you have a friend, though you know it not. But you know, it was enough. . .I was so young then. . .it was really just as much to comfort myself as you that I said it. It was when I was living with you, you were, let me see, you were in class three.' 'Did you live here with us?' said Bernhard. 'Yes, for about six months.' 'I don't remember that,' said Bernhard. 'That's strange,' said Charlotte, 'you must have been nine then.' 'I hardly remember anything,' said Bernhard. He lit a cigarette. 'Do you know,' said Charlotte, 'I really feel like a cigarette. I don't smoke, or very rarely.' He held out the packet to her and lit up for her. 'Would you like one?' he asked Camilla. 'Thanks,' she said. She looked at him while he lit it. He looked away. Bitch, he thought, just you wait. Camilla said: 'How long are you staying for?' 'Till tomorrow,' he said, then added: 'I don't know.' Then he thought: Now! – and looked at her breasts. Then he pushed back his chair and rose. Without looking at anyone he pushed the chair in and went out. I did it, he thought, I did it. He went up to the attic, took off his black suit and lay down on the bed, and there he took her by force.

Bernhard woke from a dream. The sun shone straight into the room. He got dressed and opened the door. All was quiet. He went downstairs. The garden door was locked. He unlocked it and went out. The air was quite still but a large cloud hung over the mountain in the east. He sat down at the iron table and watched it. It did not come any nearer. He thought: everything seems as it used to be, as if nothing had happened.

A little later, while he was still sitting there looking at the cloud which didn't come any nearer, he heard steps behind him. It was Marion. 'So here you are,' she said. 'That cloud has been in the same place for nearly half an hour,' he said. 'We could do with a little rain,' she said. 'It doesn't move,' he said. Marion put a finger in her mouth and held it up in the air. 'There's no wind,' she said. They sat quiet for a while. 'Would you like anything?' she said. 'What?' he said. 'A glass of wine?' she said. 'Yes, please,' he said. She stood up and went in. He put a finger in his mouth and held it up in the air. 'I think she wants to talk,' he thought.

She came out with a bottle of wine and two tall-stemmed glasses. 'Such fine glasses,' he said. 'Oskar gave them to me,' she said. I won't talk about Oskar he thought. They drank. Bernhard lit a cigarette. 'You left the table so suddenly,' said Marion, 'was anything wrong?' 'No,' he said, 'I just got a splitting headache.' 'Aunt Charlotte asked me to give you her love,' said Marion. He laughed. Then he said: 'She is the eldest in the family and the next to die, she said, and she goes to one funeral after another, and her budgies died because they ate their young.' Marion smiled. 'She's sweet,' she said, 'she's like Mother.' Bernhard said: 'She told me she lived here for six months once when Mother was ill.' 'That's right,' said Marion, 'it was the year I started school. Mother was in hospital.' 'What was the matter with her?' 'I don't know exactly, something to do with her nerves.' 'It seems odd I don't remember it,' said Bernhard. 'You probably didn't miss her,' said Marion. He didn't reply. He drank. Marion filled up his glass. 'Do you often get headaches?' she said. 'No,' he said. 'Well, now and then.' He threw away his cigarette and lit a new one. 'Look,' he said, 'the cloud still hasn't moved.' 'Camilla said you're leaving tomorrow,' said Marion. 'Yes,' he said. 'What a pity,' she said. 'I have to get back to work,' he said. He drank. 'That's good wine,' he said. After a while he shot a glance at her; she sat looking down at her lap shaking her head almost imperceptibly. At length she said, not looking up: 'I don't think you want to talk, do you?' 'I am talking,' he said. 'You know quite well what I mean,' she said. He made no reply. 'I was so glad you came,' she said, 'but perhaps you didn't notice that.' He didn't say anything. He didn't know what to say. Then he said: 'I only came for your sake. I thought...' He stood up. 'Don't go,' said Marion. 'I'm not going,' he said. 'What did you think?' she said. He didn't answer. After a while he said: 'I can't help being the way I am. If I killed someone, for instance, I couldn't help it, but I won't kill anyone because I'm not like that. Everything I do, I do because that's how I am, and it's not my fault that I'm like that. Other people can say what they like. Do you understand?' He grasped his glass and drank. Then he lit a cigarette. He went over to the flowerbed, stood there looking down at the dry earth. Then he looked at the cloud over the mountain; he felt it had grown smaller. He turned towards Marion; she sat bent over, turning her glass round and round on the table. He went and sat down. 'I can be beside myself, too,' she said. 'Yes,' he said. 'But it will probably be better for you now.' She looked at him. 'Now Father is dead, I mean.' 'But Bernhard!' she said. He laughed. 'All right,' he said, 'we won't say any more about that. I'll go and water the flowers.'

Later, while they were having dinner, a wind sprang up and made the curtains flap, and when they left the table there was a flash of lightning. Bernhard went out to the garden. The sun shone but the northern sky was dark and he heard faint thunder. He sat down at the iron table; he sat with his face to the north waiting for the rain. Lightning flashed again, and he thought: like lightning from a clear sky. Then he thought: but surely that's impossible, lightning from a clear sky is impossible. At that moment Marion called his name. She stood in the doorway. 'I'm just going over to Camilla's for a while,' she said, 'are you going to stay here?' He nodded. She waved and went away. A few minutes later he stood up and went in. He called her name. Then he went upstairs and into Marion's room. The bed was made and there were no clothes lying on the chairs. He went over to the chest of drawers and stayed there looking at the photograph of their parents. He thought: I'm more like him than Mother. He stayed there in front of the photograph a while longer. Then he pulled out the top drawer of the chest, looked into it and shut it again. He just did that. Then he did the same thing with the next drawer down, and then the one next to the bottom drawer. The bottom one was locked. There was no key. He pulled out the drawer next to the bottom one and put it on the floor, and through the opening he could see a notebook, a bundle of letters tied with string, two little boxes, a wallet and a glasses case. And slightly apart, on the right, a diary. He put his hand in and picked up the bundle of letters; they were all addressed to their father; he put them back. He looked at the open door and listened, then he picked up the wallet and opened it. There were seven 1000 kroner notes in it, otherwise nothing. He put it back exactly where it had been. He picked up the diary; underneath it was a porno magazine. He opened the diary, it was Marion's. He put it back again and lifted up the drawer, stood holding it a moment, it was full of underclothes, then put it down again. He picked up the diary, leafed through it backwards to the last entry. Wednesday 17th August: Bernhard came, I had not expected that. I felt so terribly sorry for him, even though I don't know if there is any need to. He asked both Oskar and Camilla how well they had known Father. Camilla says there's something almost creepy about him, for instance about the way he laughs, but Oskar says he seems just like a perfectly ordinary person. He probably wants to comfort me.

Bernhard shut the diary and placed it so that it covered the porno magazine, then he pushed the drawer in and went quickly out of the room and down the stairs. He stopped in the hall and lit a cigarette. He opened the front door and went out on to the steps. Like a perfectly ordinary person, he thought. Then he thought: they don't see me, no one sees me. After a while some young people came down the street; he threw away his cigarette and walked right through the house and out into the garden, he sat down at the iron table. She's sure to bring Camilla with her, he thought, so as not to be alone with me.

She did not come back before the sun had gone down and he had weeded almost the whole kitchen garden. The work had made him calm, his thoughts had led him along peaceful side-roads away from here and now, and when he heard her coming he looked up and smiled. She went right up to him. 'How well you do it,' she said in a low, warm voice, and he felt a wave rising inside him. 'Yes,' he said. She stayed where she was, did not say any more. The wave rolled within him. He couldn't look up. 'I'll soon be finished,' he said. 'Yes,' she said. Then she walked away.

She came out again while he stood washing his hands under the hose. She carried a bottle of wine and two tall-stemmed glasses. They sat in the twilight sipping the wine and exchanging small talk. Darkness fell. 'It hasn't rained,' said Bernhard. 'It doesn't matter,' said Marion, 'now you've watered.' 'Yes,' he said. He looked at her, her features were almost extinguished by the night. She said: 'It's getting chilly. I think I'll go in. Are you staying here?' He nodded. 'A little longer,' he said.

GREECE

Paleface

MENIS KOUMANDAREAS

translated by Ed Emery

My name's Euripides. You don't get far in life with a name like that. At best I suppose I might have ended up as a priest, or a doctor, or a writer. But I'm a barber. One of the things I've discovered as a barber is that people have this strange need to confess. They find it a lot easier unburdening themselves to a barber than they would to a psychoanalyst. Over the years I've learnt to provide a sympathetic ear for my clients, and little by little I've developed the knack of listening to their stories and being able to pass them on to others. People enjoy going to the barber's. It's good for the soul.

On this particular day it was about midday, stiflingly hot, and since I had no customers I was skimming the morning paper. The woman from the lingerie shop next door stuck her head round my shop door. She's got red hair. Just like a fox. 'Euripides, did you see that film on TV last night? I don't usually like westerns, but the actor who was playing the Paleface was something else. A pure Adonis. You don't find men like that around these days.'

She said her piece, and since I didn't even turn round to look at her she shut the door again and went. Was it just that she'd been in the mood for a chat, or was it something else? Whenever she comes poking her nose round the place, something weird always seems to happen. The other day, she'd hardly shut the door when this man turned up. He was the brother of a customer I hadn't seen for months. 'How's

Pavlos?' I asked. 'Euripides, you're going to have to come up to the house,' he said. 'We need you to shave him up there.' He was obviously very worried about something. So I went, even though I had a stinking cold and a headache at the time. And there I found my old customer, in bed, propped up on three pillows and dressed in his wedding suit. He was on his death bed! 'We want you to give him one last shave,' his brother said.

So anyway, I was thinking about all this, sitting with the newspaper across my knees, and my mind was miles away. All of a sudden something blocked out the sun. I looked up. A black shadow, standing in my doorway. For a moment I thought it was one of the crows who work in the undertaker's office down the road. I usually take a detour to avoid the place because it gives me the creeps, but if I absolutely have to pass it, I keep my fingers crossed as I go by.

Anyway, it was a young man in a black suit. I said: 'Can I help you?' His hair was the same colour as his clothes, and if it hadn't been for the bright pink of his shirt, I really would have taken him for an undertaker. But maybe he was one of the flash kids who parade round the streets in the hopes of getting lucky with the girls. He didn't say anything. He was wearing dark sunglasses, and his face was as white as a circus clown. I asked: 'Are you wanting a haircut?' What else could I have said?

He nodded and came into the shop. Straight away I found myself wishing that he hadn't come in at all. It's one thing to have a bird of ill omen sitting on your doorstep, but it's another to have it walking through your door. I got out of the way, a bit reluctantly, to let him pass.

I always say that the way a customer sits in a barber's chair speaks volumes about the kind of person he is. Some of them flop into the chair like a sack of potatoes, others perch on the edge, and others wriggle around like souls in torment. My young man first ran his finger across the chair to make sure there was no dust on it. Then he sat down, as stiff and unbending as a tailor's dummy. His suit was made of good cloth. Hand-stitched and definitely not off the peg. He had shirt cuffs. And on his wrist a gold Rolex shone, like a little sun. His nails were trimmed and filed to perfection. But they weren't the hands of an aristocrat, nor of a city boy either. His had thick veins on the back, and I reckoned that hands like that could have squeezed water out of stones.

'Won't you take your jacket off?' He hesitated. He allowed me to take it off him, though, and watched to see where I was going to hang it. In his pink shirt he looked like a wild horse at a rodeo, all decked out for the occasion. I arranged the towel round him and moved his head to get him at the right angle. I always do this with a new customer. It helps me to get a sense of how he likes things done – whether he'd like me to hurry and be done with it, or whether he'd prefer me to take my time.

With this one I might as well have saved myself the effort. He sat there, stiff as a post and all bottled up inside himself. Apart from his paleness, what most struck me was the amount of hair he had. I don't often get customers with hair like that. Even with younger men with a fair head of hair I can always spot the start of a bald patch. But this one's hair would have lasted for a hundred years – always assuming, of course, that he lived that long. 'Will you take your sunglasses off?' I asked. He hesitated again. It was as if I'd asked him to remove his trousers. Still, since I insisted, he took them off and tucked them into his shirt. His eyelids were like heavy curtains covering his eyes. Did he have any particular preference? 'A trim and a general tidy-up,' he said, 'that'll do fine.' He spoke in a low voice, and slightly out of breath, as if he'd been running.

His previous barber must have been an amateur, because his hair was in a terrible state. I couldn't help passing comment: 'Good God, what have they done to you, son?' His eyes looked up, black and sharp. He had the kind of eyes that look even more attractive when they're tired. Beauty's a strange thing: an ugly face can't become any more ugly, but a good-looking face is capable of looking ever more beautiful.

As time went by, I began to become aware that behind his impeccable appearance lay some hidden exhaustion. Either physical or psychological, I wasn't sure which, although often the two go together. 'Would you like a coffee?' I asked. He was about to say no, but when I added, 'I'll have one too,' he said simply, 'thank you.' I thought maybe I'd been a bit harsh on him. This young man – he couldn't have been much older than twenty-five – was probably on his way home from some very hard job, and hadn't had a chance to catch up on his sleep. Maybe behind his stiff, wooden manner there was a very proper person. Maybe even sensitive.

'Your job must be very tiring,' I said, addressing him in the informal form. Given his age, he could almost have been my son. 'Yes, very,' he said, with a sigh. He'd budged a bit, at last. 'I hope it's not too hard,' I said. He looked at me inquiringly, as if trying to get the measure of me. He was a very cautious young man. Who knows, maybe very clever too. 'Unless of course you're not coming from work,' I continued. 'It's work,' he said curtly. I drank a sip of my coffee and set to work on his sideburns. 'Do you want them trimmed back?' I asked. Some people like their sideburns long, and others prefer them close-cropped like soldiers'.

'Any way you think a woman would like them,' he replied, without pausing for thought. 'So that's it!' I thought. He's on his way to a woman. Strange, though, because usually people are tired *afterwards*. What wouldn't I have given to be twenty-five again! I said: 'Women tend to like them about halfway; they go for the average.' 'And mediocrity too, sometimes,' he replied, puckering his lower lip. 'Imagine it,' I said, 'if there weren't any women... we men would be out of a job.' He seemed to go cool on me. I paused with my scissors. 'Don't get me wrong...' I said. 'We're men of the world... some things can be said between men.' He didn't react.

'You haven't finished your coffee,' I said, trying to change the subject. 'I don't want any more,' he replied. 'Coffee makes me edgy. Anyway, I'm short of sleep.' 'So that's it,' I thought, 'that's the reason why he's so pale.' 'Do you work nights?' 'Sometimes nights, sometimes days.' By now I'd slowed down the haircut, because even though he didn't necessarily want it that way my curiosity was getting the better of me. 'Does that mean you have two jobs?' He smiled derisively. 'I'd be a lot better off if I did,' he said, loosening the towel from around his neck. 'I have to keep running just to stand still.' 'Is it too tight?' I asked, and as I loosened the towel I sensed that he was poised on the edge of my trap. Maybe his job was just something run-of-the-mill, but then again maybe it was something really interesting.

He didn't speak again until I'd finished. I helped him on with his jacket, and he put on his dark glasses again. He stood up for me to give him a brush-down. 'Black clothes pick up dirt as easily as white clothes,' I said. 'The same goes for women,' he said, simply. 'Black or white, they all mark the same.' 'Are you married?' I asked. He gave me a sideways look as if to say: 'Do I look it?' 'I hope I'll be seeing you again,' I said, in an effort to break the silence. 'Always assuming you like the haircut, of course, and that you don't have a regular barber of your own.' On this I had my doubts. He took a quick look in the mirror. 'I don't. I get my hair cut wherever I happen to be at the time.' 'Ha,' I laughed, 'I know, you must be a travelling salesman... selling something pretty fancy and expensive? Is that why you're always on the move?' Maybe, who knows, he might finally put me out of my misery. 'You're not far off there,' he replied. But then he suddenly turned serious and unapproachable again. 'This,' I thought, 'is the kind of man who lets nobody near him except maybe his mother or his girlfriend.' 'Anyway,' I said, 'I look forward to seeing you again, because something tells me you'll be back before too long. I imagine your job needs you looking pretty smart.' 'Goodbye,' he said, all poker-faced, and turning his back on me he disappeared into the shadows of the street. Tufts of his hair lay there on my floor.

'Euripides?' It was the old woman from the shop next door. More irritating questions again. 'Have you got any coffee to spare? I was meaning to ask you, who was that young man in your shop yesterday? He was rather handsome. But I thought there was something strange about him. In fact, to tell you the truth, he had me frightened for a moment.' She looked at me, fluttering her eyelashes. 'He was an undertaker,' I said. And when she heard that she forgot all about the coffee and disappeared like a shot.

It must have been two months later; it was autumn already, and the leaves were falling from the trees. I'd cleaned down the bench and was all ready to shut up shop. Suddenly I saw that shadow outside the window again. I was almost alarmed for a moment. From the way he was peering from behind his dark glasses he looked more like a burglar checking out the premises.

I pulled myself together and opened the door. He was wearing a different suit this time, but it was as black and expensive as the last one, and he was wearing a violet shirt, open at the neck. You could see his neck, the dimple under his Adam's apple, and a bit of chest. 'Come in,' I said, ushering him in. 'I knew you'd be back.' And apart from the fact that he still looked strange, he was looking good.

This time he tossed his jacket carelessly down on to one of the chairs. I took it and hung it up carefully. He wasn't wearing a vest under his shirt, so I could see his body. White as marble. He settled into the chair with the air of a man who knew the routine. His gold Rolex was still shining like a little sun. Was it just there for show, or did he need it for his work? He glanced in the mirror and then looked away. Was it because he already knew how he looked, or was it something else, that he refused to see? There's always something mysterious about men's relationship with mirrors. He was even paler than the last time, and his cheekbones were more in evidence. 'Would you like a coffee? A sandwich?' I picked up the phone to order. He didn't say no. 'Will you take your glasses off?' He obeyed like a little boy. 'Whoever trimmed you last wasn't up to the job,' I said, as I ruffed up his hair with the comb. 'You'd be better off with a regular barber, even if he's only average, because at least he'd know your head.' That's what I advise all my customers once I've got their confidence.

I asked: 'How's your work going? I imagine it's not too bad. The autumn's usually a good time, because everyone's back after the holidays.' He shrugged. So I tried again. 'Or does your work tick over the same whether it's summer or winter?' I asked all this in a voice that was as neutral as possible, trying to get him to open up. He watched me with his slit eyes in the mirror. 'In my job,' he said, 'people need me all the year round, any time of the year.' 'What's that, then?' He laughed, but didn't rise to my question. When he laughed he lost his heavy man-of-the-world air and became like a little boy, all simplicity. But as it turned out, I was the simple one!

'Whatever your job is,' I said, 'I reckon you must do it pretty well. You can always tell the lazy bastards, even from a distance. And unfortunately nine out of ten young men of your age are just out looking for easy money.' The smile left his face. 'That's the way I was, too,' he said. 'When I left school I didn't even want to know about work. I always reckoned that what grown-ups did was just boring and pointless. And that's still the way I think. I fancied the easy life too,' he continued, 'but sometimes the easy roads are the hardest roads to travel.'

Suddenly his tongue had loosened, and I reckoned if I just pushed him a bit I might solve the mystery. 'You know best,' I said. 'At your age you must have learned something.' 'How old do you think I am?' he asked. 'Twenty-five or twenty-six.' 'Twenty-three,' he said, disappointed. 'And if I didn't work in the way I work, you'd have taken me for a schoolboy. In my family we all hide our ages.' I tried to prod him along. 'Do you live with your family?' He shook his head emphatically. 'Are you an only son?' 'I've got one younger brother – he's still at school,' and at this, for the first time, his voice sounded almost human. My scissors were working almost as fast as my brain. His last barber had perpetrated a real disaster. 'If you carry on at this rate,' I said, 'you'll end up a disaster.' He started up. I came within an ace of snipping his ear off. 'What do you mean?' 'The barbers who've been doing your hair,' I said, 'what did you think I meant. . .?' He seemed to calm down again. 'The first thing that counts in my work is looking good,' he said. 'Without that I'm nothing.' 'When a man has character,' I ventured, 'appearances come second.' He pulled a face. 'Don't pull faces like that,' I warned, 'you'll end up with wrinkles.' 'Who cares!' he shrugged. 'When you learn what I actually do for a living you won't have such a good opinion of me.' I stopped and looked him in the eye. 'What did you say your name was?' He hesitated. 'Antonis.' 'Antonis. . .' I thought, '. . .like Adonis.' 'To be honest,' I told him, 'I don't give a damn, you could be a mass murderer for all I care. All I want to know is that you're OK with me.' He laughed. 'That's exactly what my lady clients tell me.' 'Do you only have lady clients?' I asked, casually. 'Yes,' he replied, without looking at me, 'and I can never do enough to keep them satisfied.' A pain shot from my right hand right up my back. A sign of old age. 'Do you prefer dealing with women rather than men?' I asked, testing him out. 'Are they better business?' I felt as if I was tiptoeing across one of my own razors. 'They squeeze you dry,' he said. He had an air about him that was halfway between weariness and disgust. 'If I carry on like this,' he said without looking at me, 'I'll be dead set for TB and an early death.' 'What's the connection between that and your work?' He had just about slid out of the seat by now, as if he was sitting on a sloping plank. And my thoughts were slipping pretty low too. 'Not to put too fine a point on it,' he said, 'that's precisely my job: women.' I bent down to pick up my scissors. In all my years as a barber, that was the first time I'd ever dropped my scissors. 'There you are,' he said, 'I told you that once you learnt the truth you wouldn't want me for a customer.' I dipped my scissors in the jar with the alcohol. 'Shush,' I said, curtly, 'don't you realize what appalling men you've been trusting your hair to? You should have been going to the best barbers in Athens.'

I continued with his haircut, and he continued with his tale.

'I grew up in Aigaleos. By the age of fourteen I still knew nothing about anything. The bigger girls used to come round, and they'd stroke my face and finger my body. Then they'd giggle, as if they had some secret joke among them. My mother used to shout: "Get your hands off him, you horrible females," and she'd chase them away. "You'll wear the poor boy out." And then she'd turn to me: "Put some clothes on. What are you, stupid?" I started going to a gym. The gym trainer used to tell me, "You won't need to work. You've got a body that was made by God himself." My father was in the refrigerator business, and he started taking me to work with him. "So's you can learn how to earn a living," he used to say, "and stop hanging around like some street kid."

'About that time we had this woman who used to come and stay at our house. She was a distant aunt on my father's side. She lived in Patras. She had a taste for wearing silks and perfumes, and she used to leave off wearing her stockings before spring really arrived. My family didn't really approve of things like that. One evening when we were alone in the house, she started asking me in a roundabout sort of way whether I had a girlfriend, and whether I'd ever been kissed. The more questions she asked, the more tongue-tied I became. "Don't be shy, darling, it's all perfectly natural." And she'd be stroking my hair with one hand while the other was giving me a massage up and down my spine. "You should try to stop stooping," she said. "For a young man, his body is his wealth. And wherever you are," she warned, "beware of women. Keep your wits about you." I wondered why she was saying all this. She would leave the house in the evening and come back way after midnight. I'd hear the sound of her key in the door and it would wake me up, all excited. All day long my father and mother would whisper about her behind her back, but whenever I was around they'd clam up.

'One evening I heard her key in the door. For some reason it wasn't turning properly. "She can't even find the keyhole," I thought. All of a sudden I heard my parents wake up. I half opened my door. They both had hold of her, one on each side, and she was quivering like a fish. Was she having an attack or something, or was she drunk? I could see her breasts bouncing about inside her blouse. After a bit she started screeching. They shut all the doors and windows. Next morning she left, and that was the last I saw of her. But I always remember what she told me: "Beware of women, and keep your wits about you."

'I'd begun going out in the evenings. I often got back in the early hours of the morning. I was having terrible arguments with my father, and my mother used to take my side when I wasn't there. I began doing the rounds of the brothels. One time I fell in with a blue-eyed blonde. She was an angel, compared with the rest. She'd finish with her other customers and keep me till last. One day she suggested, "Let's go to my place." So we went to her house, and you know what, she gave me her day's takings for that day, and she carried on doing that for the best part of a month.'

'So, Antonis,' I asked, 'did you carry on with the whores?' 'No,' he said, 'worse than that.'

'The local police station sent for my father to go and see them. "You'd best take your son in hand. Otherwise he's going to end up in trouble." I realized that I wasn't cut out to be a pimp, so I went back to work. That was when I got my first girlfriend. A teacher in a hairdressing college. She wasn't so good-looking, but she didn't fall for me just for my looks. We used to go out together, to cinemas and cafés. She changed my hairstyle – I'd had it long, but she gave me a shorter cut. Anyway, the time came for my military service. And she was sending me letters every day of the week.'

'Where were you serving?' I asked. 'Ebro and the islands. I didn't fancy it! I went sick, and they put me on 401, and from there I got a deferment. The form had me down as "temporarily unsuited for service". I went back to my hairdresser girlfriend, and we started having rows. She wasn't so keen on me any more. Then some film producer turned up in the café where we used to hang out, in Crucifixion Square, and he started chatting me up. "Do you mind if I call you by your first name?" and all that sort of thing. He gave me a phone number where I could reach him. "You're wasting your time," I said, "I've no talent." I knew that he didn't want me for film-making, so I passed his number to a friend of mine who was into that sort of thing. That's what I mean, Euripides, all they want is my body.'

This was his misfortune; now I understood. 'So what then, Antonis?'

'I told my father I wouldn't be going back to work in the fridge business. I ended up finding a job in a textile shop in Ermou. I got the job through a small ad. There were all kinds of women passing through the place, and every once in a while they'd take me home with them, along with their rolls of cloth. There was one well-stacked forty-year-old with a hat like a chamber pot. "Are you Chinese, darling," she asked. "No," I said. "Vietnamese." She turned and said to one of her friends: "I see the boy's got a sense of humour." She bought up half the shop, and insisted that I deliver the stuff with my motorbike.

'It was a very smart house. Everyone sitting round drinking tea. A few other women turned up, all about the same age as her. They were all pinching my cheek and laughing like they were playing with fire or something. I wasn't so skinny in those days, I had a bit of meat on me. "Why don't you leave that silly job," Kyria Olympia told me. "I'll introduce you to a world that you never even knew existed." She taught me how to hold a teacup properly. "Not with your little finger sticking out. You use one teaspoon for the sugar and another for the tea, and keep your legs together when you sit down, and don't crack your knuckles, and stop writhing your neck around like that, it makes a terrible noise, what are you, a hinge? I won't have you behaving like a tramp!" For some reason they all took me for some kind of street hooligan. So why did they want me? I bided my time. My postponement ran out, and the time came for me to report back for military service.

'I went back, and they put me straight into prison. This was in Tripoli. The cold was unbelievable, and there I was, locked in a cell with some other idiots. I wrote my folks all kinds of complaining letters. "Keep your wits about you, son," they wrote, "and don't go doing anything stupid." In the end I got my discharge papers. Not very flattering – they had me down as crazy. The first day I was back in civvies, I went back to see my folks. They shut the door in my face. I rang my hairdresser girlfriend. She told me: "I can't see you, I'm up to my neck in work." So I decided to knock on Kyria

Olympia's door.

'That day there happened to be a man at her house. About forty, he was. He was wearing an Italian suit, a Dior tie and a worsted waistcoat with a watch chain to one pocket. He had a toothpick, and when he smiled you could see his gums. His teeth were rotten. He introduced himself. "My name's Agisilaos. I'm a producer." Exactly what kind of producer wasn't clear. "Where did you find this one?" he asked Olympia. "I found him in a sale," she said, and she laughed loudly. "He's all yours if you want him. I bought him for you." They were talking about me like I was an object. I swallowed my anger. Seeing that I had no work and seeing that I'd quarrelled with my folks, I ended up leaving Kyria Olympia's house with this Agisilaos.

'As we drove along in his car – he had a silver Ferrari – he said: "Why don't you come and join me in my business? You could be my stand-in on the phone." "You mean you want me as a telephonist?" "Wait a minute while I explain. When they phone, you have to be ready to go." "Go where?" "Where do you think? What are you, an idiot? To women, of course. Not the likes of Kyria Olympia, but aristocrats and jet set types." I didn't even know what "jet set" meant. "Come on," he said, "don't give me a hard time. . . As regards any money you earn, you get half and the other half comes to me, minus perks and tips of course." "How much?" I asked. "A thousand drachmas up front. That enough for you? Plus tips and so on. Mind you, I want you dressed smartly. Get your hands and feet manicured, and try a bit of circuit training." He sent me to a gymnasium in Kolonaki. "If you show willing and work hard, you could go far. Your money will go up as well. It depends on you."

'So that's how it all began. Morning, noon and night, I was on sentry duty next to the phone. Like doing my military service over again. I'd arrange the appointments, number so-and-so, such-and-such a street. . . Every kind of place you can imagine, anywhere from Glyfada to Thessaloniki, and all hours of day and night. It could be two in the morning or two in the afternoon. "Depends when they're on heat," the boss said. "After a while you'll get your own car," he said. "And if you're good at your work, you might even get your own house." I was living in a bachelor flat in Makriyanni at the time, and getting around on a motorbike.

'Up until that point,' Antonis continued, 'I'd just followed my fancy. What did it matter if a woman was getting on a bit – if she was old, even – provided I didn't have to go back and depend on my parents. But now I'd become a professional in Agisilaos's line of business. I had to be at a given place at a given time, dressed, washed and combed, because, like my boss said, "They don't want hobos coming along. Try to sound intelligent," he said, "like you've got something to say – not too much, but make it good." So I smartened myself up. I went to houses which I couldn't have imagined in my wildest dreams, with Filipinos and Albanians and Poles running around the place, cleaning, cooking and looking after the children, while the women themselves lay around making eyes at me.'

'Cheap, that's what they are, Antonis,' I said. 'Compared with them, whores are angels, don't you agree?' 'I don't know about that,' he said, 'I just get on with my work.' Once again he had that faraway look to him, like he'd just smoked half a kilo of hash. 'So how does the admin side of things work, with these women of yours?' I asked, leaning over him. I was dying of curiosity. Like being at the movies. 'First,' he said, 'you get a phone call, and the office organizes the rendezvous – always assuming that they're proper clients, and not a set-up job with the police sticking their noses in.' 'That's a point – what about the police?' I asked. 'Don't they know what's going on?' 'Of course they do, but they prefer to turn a blind eye. In return for a small consideration, needless to say. Now what about this for a story – I shouldn't be telling you this, but I think I can trust you... One time I even ended up with the wife of a police chief. They're the best.' 'That's as may be,' I said, 'but how do these women choose among you?' 'We all have ID cards with photographs, except that we use pseudonyms instead of our proper names. And if the women prefer it, there's a bar where they can come to meet us first, to get to know us, a bit like a bar in a hotel or a relax house, if you know what I mean.' 'Ah, so that's what they call them these days...' I said, '...relax houses!' 'Anyway,' he said, 'if they like you, they tell their friends about you, and they pass round phone numbers and so on, and the main thing is that everything is discreet; any woman who wants it is guaranteed complete secrecy.' 'So what are your pseudonyms?' I asked. 'Well, let's see... There's one whose nickname is "Hopalong", because he broke both his legs falling off his motorbike. Another one's called "Carditsa", because that's where he comes from – he's married, by the way. Then there's "Angel": he's called that because any woman who comes his way, he always says, "Hello, Angel!" And so on.' 'Amazing city, this Athens,' I said. 'There's progress for you!' I didn't even have to ask what his nickname was. He was Paleface to a T.

'What about your girlfriend? Did you carry on seeing her?' I asked. I wasn't expecting him to say yes. 'What do you expect from a hairdresser?' he said. 'Don't get me wrong... She always wanted the last word. I got shot of her. I may be mad, but she was crazy.' 'Never mind, you'll find another one soon enough.' And so saying I lifted a couple of fingers of his hair to measure it with my eye.

'One day they sent me to the airport to pick up a parcel, and I ran across this air hostess. She was about the same height as me, with long, wavy hair and a brilliant body. She'd just come off a flight, and she was in the passenger toilets, changing out of her uniform. Something clicked between us. I took her from behind, like a dog, though that's not usually the way I'd do it. It was like she'd hypnotized me – the way she moved, the way her hair moved as she walked, the shape of her waist... this was a woman!

'I caught up with her outside, at the bus stop. "No need to wait for a bus," I said. "I've got a car." I had the silver Ferrari. "Your own?" she asked. "My own," I replied. That same evening we went to a restaurant and a disco, and needless to say we ended up back at her place. She had a proper fireplace and a bed the size of an airfield. It just so happened that both of us had the next day off. If there's anything worth waiting for in life, Euripides, it's days like that, wouldn't you say?' 'What was her name,' I asked, 'if you don't mind my asking?' He hesitated for a moment. 'Olga,' he said. 'I don't know why, but I always had the impression that she was giving me a false name. I suppose in her position I'd have done the same.' 'Was she blonde or brunette?' I asked. 'A redhead,' he replied. 'Bad sign...' I thought, as I brushed the trimmed hair off the back of his neck. 'The best thing about her,' he joked, 'was that even though she was always up in the air somewhere, she never got ideas above herself.'

'Antonis,' I said, leaning over him, 'can I ask you something? Does she know what you do for a living?' He glanced at me as if to say: 'You must be joking!' 'But doesn't she have her suspicions?' 'She's completely wrapped up in her job – one minute she's flying to Amsterdam, the next it's New York, and in between, when we have time between her flights and my massages, we stay at home and light the fire. I like that. It feels like I belong to a family. It feels like coming home to my mother.' 'How old is she?' I asked. 'Thirty.' 'When women say thirty, write thirty-five. Don't you ever go with younger girls, Antonis?' 'No – kids are just a nuisance. Older women know what they want.' 'And in the meantime,' I said, 'I presume you moved to a new house and bought yourself a palace.' 'No,' he said, 'I've still got my bachelor flat in Makriyanni, and a secondhand sports car that

I bought to get around with. Otherwise people give you funny looks and judge you by the kind of car you've got.'

'Can I ask something else, Antonis?' He looked at me as if to say: 'Seeing that we've come this far, fire away...' 'How does it work with the money side of things? Do they pay you cash, or what?' 'The office pays me on a weekly basis. Fifty-fifty, like I told you.' 'And what about the women?' I asked. 'Do they give you tips?' 'Only in the form of little presents,' he said. 'Whatever takes their fancy.' He spoke with the slight resentment of an offended beggar. 'But,' I said, 'how do you manage things with your girlfriend, Olga? Aren't you always worn out from being with the others?'

I wondered whether he was losing patience with me, but it seemed like he'd been bitten by the confession bug. I, for my part, was all ears. 'Any woman's going to stick with a man who gives her satisfaction,' he said. 'I don't doubt that,' I said, 'but are you still enjoying yourself with her? I hope you don't mind my asking.' 'To tell you the truth,' he said, 'at the start I felt as if I was making love with one of my own kind, somebody whom I'd chosen myself. But little by little, she became a habit too. I began to lose the taste for it. Needless to say, she noticed, and she got angry.' 'So what do you do now?' 'I shut my eyes and think of other women. Different women. Women I've seen on the streets, on motorbikes with the wind lifting their skirts and blowing their hair. Women in the lift, squeezed up against me. Women on videos.' He had his eyelids half closed, like stage curtains concealing a porno show, and I thought, 'Well, son, with all those women... who wouldn't get tired of it!'

He glanced down at his watch. The gold Rolex. 'Are you in a hurry? One of your women?' 'I have to get back to the phone,' he said, 'Olga's going to ring today.' 'Well, if it's for Olga, I wish you luck,' I said, and I gave him a wipe behind the ears with the alcohol. 'She will insist on bringing me presents all the time, from New York, Hong Kong and so on.

And I keep telling her "Stop it, don't do that."' 'Why?' I asked, amazed. 'After all, she is your girlfriend, isn't she?' He laughed. 'But you don't understand, Euripides. When the other women are always buying me aftershaves, gold chains and rings and so on, I'll end up thinking that Olga's just like the rest of them.' Saying this seemed to relax him. I took him by the shoulders to massage him momentarily. 'And don't you ever give her little bits and pieces sometimes?' 'Of course I do,' he said. 'Apart from my clothes, the only other money I spend is on her and on Takis. The rest goes into the bank.' 'Who's Takis?' I asked. 'The little one,' he smiled. 'My kid brother.' His tiredness had softened him now, and his face was more relaxed, as if he was at home, in summertime, out in the yard, with his father, smoking a cigarette and talking about the refrigerator trade.

'Judging from what I've seen,' I said, 'I would say that your women are fortunate to have a young man like you around.' He nodded. 'The truth is, I always try to leave them satisfied. And if possible happy. It's a big deal making someone else happy.' The way he talked suggested that he hadn't had a lot of happiness in his life. I said, 'I reckon the women who come your way are pretty lucky.' He didn't reply. I suddenly wondered whether I hadn't fallen into his trap too. Because who's to say that behind those slanty eyes and the alabaster skin there wasn't a cold and calculating gigolo lurking? And it was entirely possible that he went with men too. He looked up and caught my eye. Had he guessed what I was thinking? He wasn't a silly kid, after all – he was an extremely astute young man. 'In my line of business,' he said, 'there's no space for cheating. If anything goes wrong and the management hears about it, or you get up to monkey business and somebody complains about you, the office puts you out on your ear.' 'Does that ever happen?' I asked innocently. 'Of course,' he said. 'Just like in any job, there's always thieves and wheeler-dealers. What do you expect? We've got all kinds there. Even ex-prisoners and the odd criminal or two.' 'And are there many of you working for the office, Antonis?' 'You know what?' he said, 'there are some periods when we hardly have time to keep our trousers on, and other periods when all of a sudden there are more of us than there are jobs, so we end up competing with each other.' 'I presume,' I said, 'that the older hands get first pickings.' 'Don't be too sure of that, Euripides. Some of our lads stir up vendettas, and when they happen to be in with Agisilaos there's usually trouble.'

'Well tell me this, Antonis. Does it come about that all your fellow workers are good-looking?' (I was about to say 'like you', but I held it back.) 'I don't know,' he said, and he looked down. 'Who am I to judge men's looks?' I think I'd hit on a soft point there. 'And don't you make comparisons between yourself and the others?' I continued. 'No,' he said, 'why should I worry about them? It's enough for me that I'm happy with myself.' And you could see that he meant it. 'Would you say that you're a man of principle?' I asked, to see how he'd react. 'Of course,' he replied. 'I have them from home.' 'And what do the folk at home know about what you do?' 'They think the same as what my girlfriend thinks – that I work as a model.' 'Do they really believe that?' I asked. 'Mind you, even though I am only seeing you for the second time, I'd say you're the kind of person that breeds trust.' His eyes flickered for a moment. 'Don't you be so sure, Euripides. From the moment I learned how to hide the truth, I don't even trust myself any more.' 'That's no bad thing, Antonis,' I said. 'I'm a bit that way myself. But I still say that I'm sure about you.' I sprinkled his hair with quinine and began to rub it in. 'I'm also sure,' I continued, 'that you'll be back again some day. Tell me, wouldn't you like me to have you as a regular client?' That way, I thought, I'd end up like one of his women... I almost laughed out loud at the thought. 'Would that I could,' he sighed, with closed eyes, losing himself in the smell of the quinine. 'Most times I get my hair cut anywhere I happen to be – one day it might be Kalamaki or Kyfissia, the next day I'll be up north, in Thrace or somewhere.' 'You travel up that far?' I asked. 'I thought you only went to rich people's houses.' 'There are rich people everywhere,' he replied. 'What you don't always find is *decent* people.' Then I said: 'Haven't you ever come across a woman that you really like, and she likes you, the kind of woman you'd want to get more involved with?' 'Usually I run a mile,' he said, 'but there is one that I make an exception for.' The quinine must have knocked him out, and he'd finally surrendered to me.

'There was this fifty-year-old on Papagos, she was an officer's wife. She treated me like I was her son. We didn't usually end up in bed – more often we'd just go for drives in her car so's she could talk. She wanted to know all about my life, what I was like when I was a kid, what clothes I wore, what kind of people my father and mother were, which of them I took after, and she asked about my little brother too – the lady was all questions. Just like you, Euripides.' 'And did you give her the same sort of answers you've been giving me?' He glanced up at me to see what I was getting at. 'I don't know,' he said. 'Anyway, the fact that she was interested in me won me over. It showed that she didn't just want me for my body.'

This was obviously his weak spot, his sensitive area. 'But when you *did* go to bed with her,' I asked, 'what happened then?' 'She used to enjoy taking my clothes off one by one. My shirt, my trousers, my shoes, and as she was doing it she would say: "Oh, look at the boy's shirt... oh, goodness, what lovely socks... and look at his underwear..."' 'Strange ways, some people have! Doesn't the lady have children of her own?'

'If she did, do you think she'd be getting mixed up with the likes of me?' 'I suppose not,' I said. 'Anyway, this lady of yours presumably puts money away in the bank, pays the car insurance, pays the garage, that kind of thing...?' 'Yes,' he shouted suddenly. 'All that. Since you know, why are you asking?' He was getting twitchy again. 'There's one thing I don't understand, Antonis,' I said. 'All this desire for illicit sex, where does it come from?'

'I sometimes wonder that myself,' he said. 'Since all of them are mad on money, maybe if they had less money, that might mean that they'd have fewer vices. But in most cases,' and here his voice became quieter, 'I think it's because they're eaten up by loneliness.' 'Whereas you,' I said, 'love Olga.' 'I don't know about that. I'm not sure,' he said, in a tired voice. 'In some ways I'd really rather like to settle down with a woman. But I think I'd find it hard. You see, I'm used to a different way of things.' 'You prefer putting yourself about?' I said. His shoulders started shaking slightly under the towel. It was as if he had a fever coming on, or as if he was on drugs and had missed a fix.

I continued the massage and he calmed down again. 'My dream,' he said, 'is to go to America, to start another life. From what I hear, life over there is better and freer.' 'The world over there,' I said, 'doesn't know the meaning of going down to the café, or taking a stroll, or piling everything into the VW and going off for the weekend. And how long do you reckon you'll be able to carry on with this work, Antonis?' 'The interest's piling up in the bank,' he said, 'and some day I'll have a tidy little nest-egg.' 'You're lucky, you don't have many outgoings, do you?' I said as I passed the razor over the nape of his neck like a caress. 'When the body is tired,' he said, for no apparent reason, 'the mind will know it.' All of a sudden he was talking in oracles. 'Do thoughts like that frighten you, Euripides?' 'Would it make you happier if they did? No,' I said. 'When I was young, I would have done things differently. Any male, when he's not prevented by his upbringing, is game for anything and everything.' 'Are you saying that if I was better brought up, I wouldn't be earning my living like this?' he asked tentatively, like a little boy. 'Of course,' I said, 'in that case you'd have been well brought-up, hungry and penniless!' 'And how about you?' he asked. 'Why did you become a barber?' 'So that I could make other people look good,' I said, 'seeing that I'm never going to be good-looking myself.' He looked at me with an air of puzzlement. 'Do you mind if I ask you something, Euripides?' he asked. 'What's that?' 'Can you tell me why I've been telling you all this?' 'That's why you come to me in the first place, Antonis. . .' I said, bending over him. 'You come because you *want* to tell everything. This is one of the facts of life – everybody trusts a barber. With all the things I've learnt about the lives of my customers, I could write a book.'

He put on his jacket and his dark glasses, and reached into his pocket to pay me. He looked like a proper young man now, although still as thin and pale as before. He wasn't quite so twitchy. He looked as if the confession had done him good. Everything disappears one day, I thought – youth, beauty, and you wind up with no friends, no relations and just the skin you stand up in. And maybe no god either. He put his hand into his pocket. He earns his money, easy come, easy go, I thought. 'And if you don't go abroad, Antonis, what will you do then?' 'What else?' he said. 'I'll go back to Aigaleos. I'll set up business there.' 'Why Aigaleos?' 'That's my home,' he said. 'That's where I belong.'

I saw him to the door. The autumn light softened his features, but he was still looking pale and wistful. I watched after him as he disappeared into the shadows again. It still surprises me that he'd told me all that – it was as if he'd had it all bottled up inside him. For all that he looked as light as air, his spirit was heavy. When society abolishes work and people devote themselves to their true nature, then maybe there's hope that the world will be a better place, and people won't feel the need to break the law. But supposing there's something in people's nature that makes them want to be gigolos, I thought. . . What if that's the only way that they can find themselves, the only way they can express themselves...? Isn't that the way with all the world's artists too? Aren't they lawbreakers and taboo-breakers too? He was an artist, I concluded, in his own way.

It was eight in the morning, and I'd just opened. The middle of winter, with a wind that must have been blowing straight from Siberia. When the weather's like this, I tend to think gloomy thoughts. Perhaps that's why I wasn't surprised when I saw his shadow again, and then saw him coming into the shop. He was dressed all in black from head to toe, with a white shirt. Who knows, maybe in the meantime he really had become an undertaker. He removed his dark glasses without a word – I decided that he probably wore them at night too – and slipped into the chair like it was familiar territory. This time he didn't take his jacket off, and I noticed that it needed a good brush around the shoulders. 'Dandruff?' I asked. He didn't reply. His hair was in pretty bad shape, his face was looking paler than before and his eyes were looking sunken and defensive. 'Shall I order coffee? I'll order anyway – you don't have to drink it if you don't want it.' I asked him how business was. As if he was running a barber's shop! And he asked me how I was doing for clients – as if I was a prostitute! I noticed that he wasn't wearing cuffs. 'Where's your watch?' I asked. 'I got shot of it,' he said, monosyllabically. When the coffee arrived, he wouldn't touch his. 'No thanks, Euripides, I've cut out coffee and cigarettes. Doctor's orders.' 'A doctor at your age?' I was puzzled. 'At first I found it strange too, but I haven't been feeling too well recently.' 'You're looking tired,' I said, 'you should take a break or something.' I cut his hair in silence, and he was equally uncommunicative as he sat there.

'I wanted you to do my hair for the last time,' he said after a while. 'I have to go into hospital for tests tomorrow.' I felt shivers running down my spine. There must have been a draught coming in somewhere. Maybe I'd left a window open. 'I don't fancy putting myself in the hands of hospital barbers,' he continued. 'They're just nurses who happen to pick up a pair of scissors once in a while.' 'Why do you wear a black tie?' I asked. I'd been dying to ask him this right from the start. 'My father died.' 'I'm sorry to hear that... Was he old?' 'Coming up for seventy; I doubt that any of us is going to live that long.' What did he mean by that 'us'? Himself and his friends working at the office? 'Don't ever say that again,' I said. 'You're looking splendid. With the progress of medicine these days, you'll live to be a hundred.' He looked at me quizzically. 'Can't you see I'm in a state? The day before yesterday I even had to cancel two appointments.' 'Is that the first time it's happened?' 'The second. And I don't want it to happen a third time, so that's why I'm going for these tests.' 'Couldn't you have had them done by your local doctor?' 'I did. They said I had a low blood count and too many white cells.'

'So what exactly seems to be the matter with you, Antonis?' I asked, gently, so as not to make him defensive. 'I feel kind of listless, and I've lost weight too. And at night I'm always having this dream, somebody with a key, trying to find the keyhole, and not being able to.' We looked at each other. I always find that I establish the best understandings with my customers through eye contact. 'How's your girlfriend?' I asked, in an attempt to change the subject. 'She's flying to New York today; if it hadn't been for her, I think I'd have killed myself.' 'What sort of things do you talk about?' 'Forty Second Street, Times Square, the Mississippi, the cotton fields... she knows it all inside out.' 'And isn't she worried about the state of your health?' 'I can't bring myself to tell her the truth.' Imagine it, he was ashamed to tell her that he was ill, but he wasn't ashamed to tell me. 'What about your mother? You should tell her at least.' 'She's only just getting over my old man's death.' 'And Agisilaos?' 'He has no idea. I asked him for a fortnight off for family reasons, and he said: "What? Again?"' 'And what about Takis,' I asked, 'your kid brother.' 'He's the last person I'd want to worry,' he said.

The conversation was getting a bit heavy. Winter isn't the best time for discussions like this. 'You've been working too hard,' I told him. 'In a month or so you'll be right as rain. And don't you start going to any other barber,' I joked. 'You come to me, if you want to look handsome.' 'Handsome?' he said, sarcastically. 'Shame you can't do anything about my health. . .' Bending over him, I brought my face close to his. Humanity sees itself in the mirror and doesn't recognize itself. 'Listen,' I said in his ear, 'I don't know how they do things in America, but in Greece your barber is like a doctor, do you hear?' 'I don't see why you're worried about me,' he said, 'this is only the third time that you've ever seen me.' 'I'll see you plenty more times yet, and don't forget, we're friends, now.' At this point I think he was beginning to get a bit dewy-eyed.

'Euripides, can I ask you a favour?' 'Go ahead.' 'Give me your phone number, so that when I go into hospital, that way I'll have someone to talk to if I want to, you know what I mean?' Of course I knew what he meant. 'Sure I'll give you my phone number,' I told him, 'but you're not going to need it. In no time at all you'll be back with your women. Like a pasha with his harem.' I don't know how I let that slip out. A look of horror passed across his face. I grasped him by the shoulders. 'And if I say things like that, it's just because we're men of the world, so we can be up front about things, can't we, Antonis?' 'My name isn't Antonis,' he said.

'Whatever your name is,' I told him, as I brushed him down, 'for me, it makes no difference.' I hurried to get his haircut over with, and said goodbye in a quiet voice. He took out the money to pay me. 'Don't worry about that for the moment, friend; you're going to have plenty of expenses now – tests, hospital and all that – you can pay me next time.' 'In my line of business we don't give credit,' he said, 'and the same goes for yours.' So saying he slipped the money into the top pocket of my jacket. I saw him to the door. 'And don't be shy about picking up the phone,' I shouted down the road after him. I watched as he disappeared in the crowd. Everyone wearing overcoats, their breath turning to vapour in front of them, and him just wearing his suit and looking as thin as a rake.

A few weeks passed. Next door, in the undertaker's, there were customers going in every day and never coming out again. Nobody came out of my shop either, on account of the fact that nobody was coming in either. No business. All of a sudden, the phone rang. Always makes me jump when the damn thing rings. But on this particular day it was like an electric shock. 'Is that Mr Euripides?' A woman's voice. Very rare for a woman to phone, in my line of business. 'It is,' I confirmed. 'With whom do I have the pleasure of speaking...?' 'I've been asked to send you something. A package. I wonder, could you tell me your address?' 'Who's the package from, might I ask?' 'It's from a customer of yours.' 'And who might you be?' 'An acquaintance of his.' A waste of time my pressing her further. Secretive. So we left it at that.

I'd forgotten all about the phone call. It was spring already, with a sun that tickled your whiskers. One lunchtime the postman knocked at my window. Three knocks – like the knock of fate, as they say. 'Euripides, there's a packet for you.' I signed the receipt. The package was neatly tied with string. It came to rest on my counter, looking at me challengingly. I waited for the last customer to leave.

Just as I was about to open it, the old vixen from next door stuck her snout round the door. There's nothing worse than somebody interrupting just as you're settling down to something. 'Good afternoon, Euripides. Spring's here. What a lovely sunny day.' And she stood there balanced on one leg like a stork. 'Did the postman find you? He was looking for you all morning.' I looked at her, not saying a word. 'Is anything the matter?' she asked. 'Can I do anything for you?' Again I didn't say a word. 'Tell me, how's that customer of yours? You know the one... It's been months since he was last here.' Her eyes were firmly on the package. 'Here, look, here he is,' I said, and I took out the contents and waved them before her eyes. It was a tuft of his hair. And as she backed off, looking alarmed, I locked the door, giving the key two turns in the lock.

Outside it was spring. The sun was shining like a gold Rolex.

About the authors

Kjell ASKILDSEN Born in Mandal in 1929, he is best known as an author of short stories, such as his collections, *Heretter følger jeg deg helt hjem* (1953) and *A Sudden Liberating Thought*, published in English in 1994. The latter won the Riksmål Prize in 1987 and the Aschehoug Prize in 1991. He is the author of several novels and was awarded the Critic's Prize twice, first with *Thomas F's siste nedtegnelser til almenheten* (1983) and then again with *Et stort øde landskap* (1992). His work has also been dramatized and filmed. Nomination for the Nordic Council's Literature Prize in 1991 confirmed his position as one of Scandinavia's most celebrated contemporary writers.

Henning BOËTIUS Born in 1939 on the North Sea island of Föhr, he completed a doctorate on Hans Henny Janhn's *Fluß ohne Ufer* and worked as editor on the complete works of Clemens Brentano. Opting for a nomadic lifestyle, he travelled extensively throughout Ireland, Scotland and Scandinavia working as a musician, painter and goldsmith. Since 1984 he has concentrated on writing. His work includes plays for radio and theatre, poems and many biographies, including *Schönheit der Verwilderung. Das kurze Leben des Johann Christian Günther; Der Gnom. Ein Lichtenberg-Roman; Lauras Bildnis* and *Joiken.*

Paola CAPRIOLO was born in Milan in 1962. She is the

author of three novels: *Il nocchiero* (1989) for which she won the Rapallo Prize, *Il doppio regno* (1991) winner of the Grinzane Cavour Prize and *Vissi d'amore* (1992), a variation on the theme of Puccini's *Tosca*, to be published by Serpent's Tail. She has also published a collection of fables, *La ragazza dalla stella d'oro* (1991) and a volume of short stories, *La grande Eulalia* (1988), that won her the Giuseppe Berto Prize. She has translated Thomas Mann and Goethe. In 1991 she was awarded the Forderpreis from Bertelsmann Buchclubs.

Atte JONGSTRA Born in Terpwispel, Friesland, he graduated in Literary History at the City of Amsterdam University in 1982. His first book *De psychologie van de zwavel* was awarded the Geertjan Lubberhuizenprijs for literary débuts and shortlisted for the AKO – Literary Award, his collection of short stories, *Cicerone*, has been longlisted for the 1994 prize. He has written two novels, *Groente* (1991) and *Het Boek M.* (1993), and has edited a collection of Dutch poetry *Dichten over Dichten*. Jongstra works as an editor for *Optima* magazine and reviews for leading Dutch publications.

Nuno JÚDICE was born in the Algarve in 1949. His first publication was a selection of poetry entitled *Obra poética 1972–1985*. His is the author of many works of poetry for which he won the D. Diniz Poetry Prize and the PEN Club Poetry Prize in 1986. His works of fiction include *Amanta religiosa* (1982), *Adágio* (1989), *Plâncton* (1991) and *A roseira de Espinho* (1994). He is a literary critic and a teacher at the University of Lisbon.

Menis KOUMANDAREAS was born in Athens. After years of working for an insurance company, he published his first collection of short stories, *Pin-ball Machines*, in 1962. He then was awarded the National Book Award for his novel, *Glass Factory* (1972). His other works include *The Barber Shop*

(1975), *The Handsome Lieutenant* (1982), *Seraphin and Cherubim* (1981) and *Vest N9* (1986). *Koula* (1978) was made into a film for television. He has also translated many authors, including Lewis Carroll and William Faulkner, into Greek

Brian LEYDEN was born in Roscommon in 1960. He won the RTE Francis McManus Short Story Award in 1988 and then the *Ireland's Own* short story competition in 1989. He also devised and performed a one-man stage show on W.B. Yeats called *Experiments in Magic*. He has taken part in a series of readings as part of the Belfast Festival at Queen's University and in a number of radio programmes. He has contributed, as writer and editor, to *Force 10* literary magazine and his RTE radio documentary, *No Meadows in Manhattan* (1991), won a Jacobs Award. *Departures* (1992), a short story collection, is his latest publication.

Javier MARÍAS was born in Madrid in 1951. His first two novels, *Los dominios del lobo* (1971) and *Travesia del horizonte* (1973), were followed by a series of prose and poetry translations from English for which he won the National Prize for Translation in 1979. He is the author of five novels, of which *El hombre sentimental* (1986) won the Herralde de Novela Prize and *Todas las almas* (1989) won the Ciudad de Barcelona Prize. He is the author of two books of essays and one collection of short stories *Mientras ellas duermen* (1990) and has had two English translations, *All Souls* (1992) and *A Heart So White* (1994). He has held academic posts in Spain, the United States and in Britain, where he was a Lecturer in Spanish Literature at Oxford University.

Ib MICHAEL was born in Roskilde in 1945. He graduated in American Indian Languages and Cultures from the University of Copenhagen in 1972. He is the author of eight novels including *En hidtil uset drøm om skibe* (1970), *Hjortefod* (1974),

Kilroy, Kilroy (1989), *Den tolvte rytter* (1993), two radio plays, a children's book, two poetry books and has translated and rewritten the Quiché-Mayas' folk book *Popol Vuh* (1975). He was awarded the Otto Gjelsted Prize (1978), the Golden Laurels (1990), the Danish Critics' Prize (1991) and the Søren Gyldendal Memorial Prize (1993) and has also taken part in many expeditions and voyages.

Michèle ROBERTS was born in Hertfordshire in 1949. A leading figure in a new generation of women writers she is the author of seven novels including *The Book of Mrs Noah* (1987), *In the Red Kitchen* (1990) and *Daughters of the House* (1992), two collections of poetry, *The Mirror of the Mother* (1986) and *Psyche and the Hurricane*, and short stories, many of which are published in the collection *During Mother's Absence*. *Daughters of the House* was shortlisted for the 1992 Booker Prize and won the 1993 W.H. Smith Literary Award. Michèle Roberts, who lives in London, reviews for *The Observer* and *The Independent on Sunday* and for BBC radio and television.

Annie SAUMONT has published twelve collections of short stories. She was awarded the Goncourt de la Nouvelle prize in 1981 for *Quelquefois dans les cérémonies*. In 1991 she received the Grand Prix de la Nouvelle de la Société des Gens de Lettres for *Je suis pas un camion* as well as the Prix Nova for her short stories as a whole. Her stories have appeared in magazines and newspapers in France, Switzerland and Quebec. Her latest collection, *Les violà quel bonheur* was published in 1993. *Je suis pas un camion* is published in the U.K. as *I'm No Truck* (Marion Boyars, 1993). Annie Saumont lives in Paris and is a widely respected translator.

Ana Luisa VALDÉS was born in Montevideo, Uruguay in 1953. After four years in jail for political reasons she moved to

Sweden in 1978. She is a graduate in Social Anthropology from Stockholm University and is currently doing feminist research there. She has won many writing competitions with her poetry and short stories and her works have been translated into Dutch, German, French and English. Her writings include *Albatrossernas krig* (1983), *Inkräktaren* (1985), *Efter Alicia* (1986) and *Väktaren* (1992). She has edited two anthologies, *Women Tales from the South* and *Jag älskar dataspel*, and has contributed to a previous Serpent's Tail anthology, *Columbus' Egg*.